His eyes fasten

cleavage...

then her face. Grinning, Jackson said, "It's a pleasure *seeing* you. I look forward to next time."

Sunni was outraged. And dangerous or not, this man needed to know she wasn't going to go down easy. He also needed to know there was more beneath her red silk dress than a memorable set of bubbles. She had long legs that could run a six-minute mile. And she was no slouch on the firing range with her .22 automatic.

Chin raised, Sunni corrected, "You mean meeting me, don't you...Jackson?"

Undaunted by her challenge, his grin opened up. "Yes. That, too."

Dear Reader,

The warm weather is upon us, and things are heating up to match here at Silhouette Intimate Moments. Candace Camp returns to A LITTLE TOWN IN TEXAS with *Smooth-Talking Texan*, featuring another of her fabulous Western heroes. Town sheriff Quinn Sutton is one irresistible guy—as attorney Lisa Mendoza is about to learn.

We're now halfway through ROMANCING THE CROWN, our suspenseful royal continuity. In Valerie Parv's *Royal Spy*, a courtship of convenience quickly becomes the real thing—but is either the commoner or the princess what they seem? Marie Ferrarella begins THE BACHELORS OF BLAIR MEMORIAL with *In Graywolf's Hands*, featuring a Native American doctor and the FBI agent who ends up falling for him. Linda Winstead Jones is back with *In Bed With Boone,* a thrillingly romantic kidnapping story—of course with a happy ending. Then go *Beneath the Silk* with author Wendy Rosnau, whose newest is sensuous and suspenseful, and completely enthralling. Finally, welcome brand-new author Catherine Mann. *Wedding at White Sands* is her first book, but we've already got more—including an exciting trilogy—lined up from this talented newcomer.

Enjoy all six of this month's offerings, then come back next month for even more excitement as Intimate Moments continues to present some of the best romance reading you'll find anywhere.

Leslie J. Wainger
Executive Senior Editor

Beneath the Silk

WENDY ROSNAU

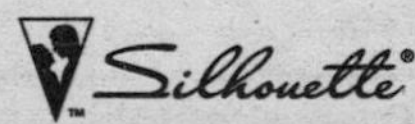

INTIMATE MOMENTS™

Published by Silhouette Books

America's Publisher of Contemporary Romance

ISBN 0-373-27227-8

BENEATH THE SILK

This edition published by arrangement with Harlequin Books S.A.

Visit Silhouette at www.eHarlequin.com

Printed in U.S.A.

Books by Wendy Rosnau

Silhouette Intimate Moments

The Long Hot Summer #996
A Younger Woman #1074
The Right Side of the Law #1110
Beneath the Silk #1157

WENDY ROSNAU

resides on sixty secluded acres in Minnesota with her husband and their two children. A former hairdresser, she now divides her time between her family-owned bookstore and gift shop, and writing romantic suspense.

Her first book, *The Long Hot Summer,* was a *Romantic Times* nominee for Best First Series Romance of 2000. Her third book, *The Right Side of the Law*, was a *Romantic Times* Top Pick.

Wendy loves to hear from her readers. Visit her Web site at www.wendyrosnau.com. E-mail her at cattales@brainerd.net. Or write to her at P.O. Box 441, Brainerd, Minnesota 56401.

To Tyler,
Our hearts know the truth,
and in that we are made stronger.
Walk in truth, surrounded by the light,
my son, and know you are never alone.
I love you….

Chapter 1

They called him the NOPD's loose cannon. His boss, Clide Blais, simply called him a pain in the ass. It was true that Jackson Ward hadn't *bonded* well with his police chief—after three years of working together, they were still deadlocked as to the proper conduct befitting a New Orleans homicide detective.

To back up Clide's argument, Jackson had gone through eight partners in two years before he'd found one that had stuck. But like everything in life, change is the one thing you can count on. After a year with Ry Archard, Jackson was again faced with the task of finding a partner he could work with—or more to the point, who could work with him.

Three partners had come and gone in the past three months, but still Jackson didn't blame Ry for taking the desk job he'd been offered. If he had a beautiful wife like Margo to come home to, he would have wanted out of the hot seat and better hours himself.

But the fact remained that he was still in limbo, sampling partners, hoping to find one who could appreciate his all-or-nothing, you-think-it, you-say-it approach to his job.

And that's where Jackson found himself on a hot and sticky Friday afternoon in October as he wheeled his issued cruiser into the visitors' lot at Charity Hospital, his newest recruit riding shotgun.

He parked the puke-green '96 Ford, then turned to speak to partner number thirteen. Thirteen was a bad number, Jackson mused, staring at the aging has-been who had fallen asleep. Seeing no point in waking him, he climbed out of the car and headed for the hospital.

On entering the lobby, the old memories of how much he hated hospitals hit Jackson square between the eyes. As a kid he'd spent countless hours in hospital waiting rooms with a cereal box between his knees watching cartoons—too young to understand the seriousness of his father's diabetes.

Harold Ward had been dead for fifteen years, but Jackson still hated hospitals, hated the feelings they evoked. The memories they resurrected. Only today he had no choice—last night his police chief's peptic ulcer had erupted, landing him in a hospital bed.

Inside the elevator, Jackson hung his thumbs in the back pockets of his jeans. He was tall—six foot three—with a case-hardened body and shaggy black hair that had been freshly cut that morning. He and Clide had been butting heads for two weeks, and with his suspension record being what it was, Ry had suggested that a new-and-improved look might raise Jackson's image a notch with the boss—that is, if he was willing to play suck-up to a man who clearly didn't like him, or the way he did his job.

He found Clide's room and knocked. A second later the gravelly voice inside barked, "You're late."

Jackson set his jaw, then swung open the door. "I'm not late—" his eyes found his boss slumped on the bed "—visiting hours don't start till—"

"Screw visiting hours, Ward. I got a crisis on my hands. If I could have found you last night, a black-and-white would have picked you up."

Now what? Jackson wondered. Other than Clide, he hadn't pissed anyone off for two or three days—not that he was aware of, anyway. He stepped inside and closed the door. "What's your crisis, Chief?"

"Milo Tandi. He was murdered night before last."

The name Tandi was as commonplace in Chicago as the Loop and Wrigley Field. The Tandis were also front-runners in the Chicago-Italian Organization. Jackson had gone to school with Milo and knew from personal experience that his old classmate was about as likable as fungus on a toad.

Clide poked a finger at the electronic device attached to his bed and hoisted the mattress to raise him upward. "Well, give me some background on him. Draw me a picture, Ward. Don't just stand there irritating the hell out of me."

Jackson fished in his pocket for a cigarette, then remembered hospital regulations and slid the pack back into his shirt. "Milo's thirty-four, same as me. He was born to Vito and Grace Tandi. The sole heir to the family fortune. Vito is alive, but he's been a recluse since the scandal."

"What scandal?"

"Grace was caught in bed with Vito's best friend."

"Go on."

"Frank Masado was the friend. He's also worth

millions, and connected. Some say Grace was carrying Frank's kid when Vito decided to slip her pretty long legs into a pair of concrete pantyhose and drop her off in the middle of Lake Michigan."

"He killed his wife?"

"It was never proved." Jackson grinned. "Guess Grace never popped up."

"Don't be cute, Ward. Keep going."

"Milo ran Vito's nightclubs. The Shedd, his favorite, is famous for its exotic dancers."

"So it's the usual? Prostitution? Gambling? Drugs? Tough guys playing tough?"

"It's all that." Jackson narrowed his clear green eyes—eyes that had come from his Irish grandfather on his father's side. His black hair, prominent cheekbones and classic nose were gifts from his mother's Sicilian heritage. "What's this all about, Chief?"

"Someone put a hole in the middle of Tandi's forehead in an apartment at the Crown Plaza. He was found naked, tied to a four-poster bed with red silk scarves. Scarves that have been traced to Silks Inc."

"Was he offed before the fun started or after?"

"God, Ward, what the hell difference does it make?"

"Just wondered if he died happy, Chief."

"He did, if that makes any difference."

"It would to me," Jackson confessed. "This place, Silks… I've never heard of it. Is it suppose to mean something to us?"

The color drained from Clide's already pale cheeks. "It means something, all right. It means my baby girl's gotten herself in trouble in *your* town, Ward. Normally I wouldn't give a damn that some Mafia mogul's son ate a bullet. But when the evidence is pointing straight at Sunni that changes things."

"Sunni?"

"My daughter. She's been living in Chicago for the past two and a half years."

While Clide started at the beginning, Jackson sauntered to the third-story window and gazed down at the congested street traffic. The crowded city had never been a problem for him. Having grown up in Chicago, he was used to people. But it was the heat that he'd never gotten used to. That's why he'd taken Ry's suggestion and cut his hair. No, not for a second had he considered playing *suck-up,* but sweating less had definitely appealed to him.

"So you see, Sunni's the prime suspect," Clide was saying. "She started Silks six months after she moved to the city. It's one of those fancy lingerie shops. And her apartment is at the Crown Plaza. That's why Detective Williams thinks he's got his case sewn up."

"Stud Williams?" Jackson slowly turned from the window.

"What's that look mean, Ward?"

"Stud was one of my partners when I worked for the CPD."

"Well hell, that's no surprise. You change partners damn near as often as I change my shorts." Clide rubbed his gut, made a face. "Williams claims the scarves are Sunni's. I thought he meant that they came from her store, but he says they're her personal property. That she identified them and that her fingerprints were on all four scarves."

Jackson relaxed his shoulder against the wall and tried to imagine what Clide Blais's daughter looked like. He'd never seen Mrs. Blais, but Clide was five foot six, seventy-five pounds overweight, and the only place he could grow hair was on his upper lip.

"Williams also told me the only reason Sunni hasn't been arrested is that she's got an alibi for the night of the murder."

"At least that's something."

"You won't think so once you hear who it is. Sunni's alibi is Frank Masado's son. The oldest one. Williams says Joey Masado is my daughter's boyfriend."

Jackson winced. "You're telling me she's been seeing both Joe and Milo Tandi at the same time?"

"Hell, no. That would be stupid."

Deadly was a better word, Jackson thought. Just ask Grace Tandi.

"Masado claims Sunni was having dinner with him in his suite when Milo Tandi took the hit." Clide rubbed his gut again, the obvious strain of the situation adding to his chronic ailment. "It's bad, ain't it? She's in deep, and it'll take a miracle to pull her out of this quicksand mess she's gotten herself into without dragging her face-first through the mud."

"If she's innocent, then—"

"Of course she's innocent. Only…"

"Only what?"

"I've got more bad news. Sunni's store is in Masado Towers."

Jackson frowned. "You didn't know that before last night?"

"Don't look at me like I'm some negligent father. Sunni made it clear when she moved to Chicago that she was tired of living in a fish bowl. Asked her mother and me to give her some space. We agreed that being the police chief's daughter had stifled her some. We phone back and forth. We're planning a trip up there for Christmas.'' Clide paused. ''I know you and I haven't seen eye-to-eye too often, Ward. Hell, maybe never. But whether I like it or not, you're *the man.*''

''*The man?*''

''You know how to get around department bureaucracy better than anyone I know. And you're familiar with who's who. You not only know the Tandi family, but you and the Masado boys were pretty tight, I hear. You lived in the same neighborhood, right?''

''That's true. But—''

''But nothing. I want you on this case. Back in Chicago today, Ward. Before supper if you can manage it.''

''I don't think I'm *the man,* Chief.''

''There's that look again. What you're telling me without turning over the dirt pile is that you were a pain in Mallory's ass for four years at the CPD before you became the pain in mine. Confession time, Ward. Is there bad blood between you and your ex-police chief?''

As far as Clide knew, Jackson had relocated three years ago for a change of scenery. He hadn't needed to know more then, and he didn't need to know more now. Yes, there was a problem. Only he wasn't going to turn over the *dirt pile,* as Clide called it. ''I'm NOPD, Chief. I—''

''I know what you are. You're the only man I can trust to do whatever it takes. I need a man who isn't afraid to go head-to-head with the devil if need be. That man's you.''

Jackson was sure he'd heard wrong. He'd been

called a lot of things by his boss, but the word *trust* used in the same sentence with his name… No, Clide must be on some pretty powerful painkillers.

"You heard me right. So get that dumb-ass look off your face. Yes, I *trust* you. Which isn't the same as liking you. There will be no Christmas present at the end of the year, and I'm not interested in knowing when your birthday is, or if you like white cake or chocolate."

"But, Chief—"

"Ry pointed out that he's seen you put a rat's eye out at fifty yards. That you keep your Diamondback .38 cleaner than your teeth. Which, he tells me, is saying a lot since you're obsessed with your teeth and carry a toothbrush in your back pocket wherever you go."

"But, Chief—"

"Okay, dammit! I admit you're the man I would pray to God was on the end of the rope if I found myself dangling ten stories in the air. But if you ever repeat that I'll call you a liar and have you demoted to a meter maid." Clide looked as if he were doing a math problem. "Sunni's twenty-six, Ward. She grew up a cop's kid, and that makes her smarter than most, but she's no match for a bunch of slick gangsters who've got more notches on their bedposts then I got hairs on my ass."

No, she would be no match for men who had been carrying guns in their back pockets since age fourteen, Jackson thought. Joe Cool and Nine-lives Lucky had the market on street survival. And the boys Milo Tandi had run with had no conscience.

There were plenty of reasons why Jackson should tell Clide to get someone else to pull his daughter's butt out of the fryer. But his boss was right—he would have an advantage over someone who didn't know the *boys.* He knew who was who, and where to dig. And he knew something else, too. He knew this was a golden opportunity, a chance to set things right with Hank Mallory—if that was at all possible.

"Bottom line, Ward, you're Sunni's best shot. Her only shot, the way I see it. Now, how much more stroking is it going to take for you to hop on that plane? Do you want me on my knees? If that'll make the difference, then I'll—"

"I can be there before supper."

His words had Clide sighing deeply. "All right, fine. Good."

"When did Sunni call?" Jackson asked, suddenly anxious to get out of the oven and into his favorite leather jacket. Chicago in October... Yeah, he could handle that.

"She didn't call, which doesn't make sense. I learned all of this last night from Detective Williams. Three hours later—after imagining the worst—I ended up in here. Sunni's mother is in Europe with her sister. I don't want Ellen to know about this. If we're lucky, she won't have to until it's all over. She'll be gone for four weeks."

Four weeks? "That doesn't give me much time, Chief."

"You have a knack for raising hell, Ward. And I've seen you when you get obsessed with a case. So get obsessed and raise some hell. This time you have my permission and my blessing."

"About Mac—"

"Take him with you. You know what they say about two heads."

Jackson could see all sorts of problems taking his partner to Chicago with him. But he was sure Clide wouldn't be interested in hearing a single one. "How do I handle Sunni?"

"Think of her as a member of your family, Ward. Your favorite cousin, or better yet, the sister you never had. The old cliché, guard her with your life, works for me. If it don't for you, imagine there's a crazy police chief holding a gun to the back of your head ready to blow it off the minute you screw up."

After all that, Jackson said, "That's not what I meant, Chief. Do I tell her why I'm in town? Or am I undercover?"

"Undercover would speed things up. But Sunni's safety takes priority, so it'll be your call. Sunni's no killer, Ward. Take my baby girl out of that ugly picture Williams painted me last night and I'll give you whatever it is you want. A raise. A promotion. A new partner… You name it and it's yours."

The idea of how to get close to Sunni Blais and still stay undercover for a couple of days came to Jackson on the airplane. Now, two hours after arriving at O'Hare, he stood inside the Wilchard Apartment Building across the alley from the Crown Plaza with half the battle won—old man Ferguson was still alive and the Wilchard's landlord owed him a favor.

"Never figured I'd see you again, Jackson."

Thinking much the same thing—Crammer Ferguson was at least ninety—Jackson stuck out his hand. "You get a face-lift, old man? You look twenty years younger than the last time I saw you."

"Still a smart-ass. Some things never change." Grinning, Crammer shot his bony hand across the counter and pumped Jackson's eagerly. "Ain't seen you in… Hell, how long's it been?"

"A good three years." Jackson caught Crammer eyeing Mac. He decided to forgo the introduction for now. "You got an apartment on the fourth floor that faces the alley. Is it vacant?"

"They're all vacant up there. Got pipe trouble and them damn plumbers are as independent as the no-good bankers and crooked lawyers in this city. What you want a place for? Your mama finally disown you?" Crammer's grin exposed six teeth evenly divided between his top and bottom jaw.

"We don't want to impose on Ma."

The *we* word sent Crammer's aging eyes back to Mac for a second time. "Who's that?"

"My partner."

"You got a dog for a partner?" Crammer's surprise shot his sparse white eyebrows into his wrinkled forehead. Looking back at Mac, he asked, "What happened to his ear? Looks like somebody chewed it half off."

Jackson had wondered that same thing. It had prompted him to dig up the reports surrounding Mac's five-year service to the NOPD. "A burglar," he explained, "and you're right, the guy bit a chunk out."

"God! A burglar bit your dog?"

"He's not my dog. He's my partner."

Crammer must have caught the irritation in Jackson's voice, and his eyebrows creased. "He lives with you, right?"

"That's right."

"And you feed him?"

"Don't have a choice."

"A year ago a tomcat started hanging around. A

fella asked me, is he your cat? I said no, he ain't. He said, but he lives here, right? I said, no, he's a free agent. He comes and goes. He asked what I fed him. I said, I don't feed free agents. I already told you, I don't own no cat." His point made, Crammer asked, "So, what happened after the burglar bit *your* dog?"

"Mac bit him back. The guy's missing his left ear. With two counts of burglary, and an aggravated assault charge as a prior, he sued the department."

"Bet the son of a bitch won, too."

"He did."

"Hell, them fool judges got no better sense than the crooked lawyers and lazy plumbers." With that, Crammer went back to studying Mac.

It was something that happened often—Mac drawing stares. One night, with time on his hands, Jackson had counted forty-three scars while the K-9 slept sprawled across his bed.

"He ain't ugly mean like he looks, is he?"

"Only when it's called for."

"Well behaved otherwise?"

"Damn near perfect." Jackson recited the lie stone sober. He wasn't going to mention Mac's flaws. Everybody had flaws, he silently mused, but Mac's chronic problems of late had been the reason why he'd been put on the top of the *List.*

Jackson hadn't even known the *List* existed, or what it meant, until after he'd accepted Mac as his partner. But within two days he had decided that a K-9 partner, *with problems,* wasn't for him. The next day he'd driven back to the pound, only to learn that dogs no longer of value to the department were destroyed—and since Mac topped the *List,* the only thing that stood between him and a lethal injection was Jackson.

He'd walked out of the pound minutes later and climbed back into the cruiser. He'd sat a minute, eyeing the new hole Mac had chewed in the seat while he'd been gone all of ten minutes, then he'd driven back to his apartment with his *new* partner.

"Your mama said you moved south. New Orleans, was it?"

"That's right. About the apartment?"

"Apartment 410 don't got no runnin' water at the moment. Got a nice two-bedroom on the second floor. You each could have a bed. Or is *your dog* a snuggler?"

Jackson ignored the mischief in the old man's aging eyes. "The fire escape running by the window up there would sure come in handy when Mac needs to take a leak." It wasn't an actual lie, though it wasn't the real reason he fancied that particular apartment.

"That might be so, but it ain't gonna accommodate your own nature call lessin' you plan on goin' out the fire escape with your dog."

"I'll take a look at the problem and see what I can do."

"You know about pipes and stuff like that?"

He didn't, but Jackson wanted *that* apartment. "Sure."

He watched Crammer scratch his head while he considered the offer, his rheumy eyes narrowing slightly. "I suppose you'll be expectin' a discount for your trouble."

"Seems fair."

"Can't make no money lettin' folks stay for free."

"Can't make no money sitting with empty apartments, either."

"Your mama musta washed your mouth out with soap six times a day when you was a runt. Mouthiest cop in Chicago, is what I always said. Mouthiest, but the best."

"Do we have a deal?"

"I'll need a hundred to seal it."

His cigarette pinched between his lips, Jackson peeled a hundred dollar bill out of his wallet, slapped it on the counter, then headed for the stairs. Five minutes later, Mac was slumped on a faded brown plaid couch from the seventies, and Jackson was assessing apartment 410 with a scowl.

As he headed into the kitchen, he pointed his finger at Mac. "No holes, understand? None of this is ours. And even if it does looks like hell, I don't want it looking worse."

After examining the kitchen and finding it had all of the necessities to keep him from starving—a noisy refrigerator, a yellow-stained sink and an old electric stove with two burners that still worked—Jackson entered the bedroom. The room was as sparse as the rest of the apartment—a narrow closet, a double bed and another floor lamp like the one in the living room with a water-stained blue shade.

The bonus was the wooden desk and chair—free of teeth marks. Jackson grunted. "That won't last," he muttered, then sauntered to the window and parted the dusty beige curtains.

Across the alley stood the Crown Plaza, and on the fourth floor directly across from his bedroom window was Sunni Blais's apartment—a penthouse suite complete with a brick terrace and greenhouse. She had ultrasheer curtains covering the two sliding glass doors that led to the terrace—one door on either side of the greenhouse.

Jackson opened the window and sucked in a breath of Chicago smog. Smiling, he angled his head and let the cool air wash over his face. When he'd left three years ago, he hadn't thought about missing the city itself. At the time, all that was important was to get away from the guilt that he'd felt over Tom's death. And so he'd packed and relocated without realizing what he was leaving behind.

As he looked over the city, he plucked a cigarette from the pack in his shirt pocket, then relaxed his shoulder against the window frame. He was on his third when movement behind one of the curtains alerted him that *she* was home. He glanced down at his watch and read sixteen minutes after six. He hadn't expected to find her home this soon after work, but he'd make a note of it.

His attention back on the apartment, he was aware that Mac had entered the bedroom. A few seconds later, he felt his partner nuzzle his leg, then start licking his boot. "Knock it off, Mac. I'll get you some water and chow in a minute."

A shadow walked past the slider, a quick movement that allowed Jackson only a brief glimpse at Clide's daughter. Minutes later, she reappeared at the other slider to the left of the greenhouse. He waited, took another healthy pull off his cigarette. The curtain moved. Then there she was, as visible as a single evening star in a black sky.

She reached for the clip that held her hair off her neck. A second later, smooth black hair fell to her shoulders. A second after that, her straight white skirt went to the floor.

Jackson released a low, undulating whistle, then watched her fingers move to the buttons on her white suit jacket. He knew what was coming next. Knew he should step away from the window. Knew he wasn't going to.

Five buttons later, she sent the jacket off her shoulders, and Jackson damn near into cardiac arrest. "Oh, hell, red underwear," he moaned as raw heat attacked his groin and caught fire.

Mesmerized, he stared at Sunni Blais's long, slender legs beneath a short red slip. Then, slowly, his gaze climbed back up to appreciate the most fabulous five-star chest he'd ever seen. "Either we have the wrong Sunni Blais, or Sis is adopted," he muttered. "There's no way in hell Clide can be her father."

As if Mac was in full agreement, he angled his head and barked loudly. Twice.

Startled by the noise, Jackson jerked in surprise, then looked down at Mac, who was up on all fours wagging his tail. Without warning, he barked again. Louder this time.

Jackson gave Mac his knee, then glanced back to Sunni's apartment to find that she'd crossed her arms over her amazing breasts, her gaze searching the alley to see where the sudden noise had originated and why. When her gaze locked with his, she opened her mouth and two words came out. The first word was *Oh.* The second word was…

"Shame on you, Sis," Jackson mumbled, "that's not a nice word."

The same two words flew out again, then Sunni was gone from sight. But not forgotten—Jackson's growing problem was now full blown and painfully obvious.

There was, however, a remedy for what ailed him. He could hobble to the bathroom and take an ice-cold shower—that is, if there had been running water on the fourth floor of the Wilchard.

Chapter 2

"You lied to the police." Sunni met Joey Masado's self-assured gaze and held it. It was just before closing and she was assembling the scattered notes on her desk that she'd made for Mary, her store manager for Silks. "You know we've never dated. Much less—"

"Spent the night together? I never told the police we spent the night together."

"You implied as much."

"Then maybe this is blackmail. Maybe that's what motivated my alibi story, you think?"

"I don't know what to think, Mr. Masado." But Sunni had a feeling she was about to find out why a man she hardly knew had waltzed into the police station four nights ago and lied through his teeth to keep her out of jail.

"Call me Joey, and I'll call you Sunni. We're dating, remember?" The reckless grin that slashed across

Joey Masado's Sicilian good looks as he sauntered through the door was as unsettling as the one-inch scar high on his cheekbone. As he sat on the plush red visitor's chair in front of her desk, he snagged her small at-a-glance calendar off her desk. After studying it, his intelligent brown eyes pinned her where she sat stiff and wary. "Looks like I'm in luck... Sunni. You're free for dinner tonight."

With her black hair swept into a twist at her nape, and her curves tastefully disguised in her designer black silk suit, Sunni looked every bit the flawless, confident businesswoman—an image she had worked hard to perfect—at least on the surface. Careful to maintain that image, she tried to relax. "If we need to discuss something, now would be a better time, Mr. Masado."

"We should be seen together. It's just that simple, Sunni."

He leaned forward, replaced the calendar, then reached out and tugged on the white silk scarf tucked into the deep vee of her suit jacket. When he sat back, the scarf came loose, baring Sunni's throat and a whole lot more. Self-conscious, she squared her petite shoulders to minimize just how amazing her God-given-gift really was.

As he threaded the silk between his long fingers, Joey said, "Four of these were found at the crime scene. Your fingerprints on each one."

"My prints *would* be on *my* scarves, don't you think? The mystery isn't whose scarves were used in the murder, but how they got into that apartment when I was never there."

"It's no mystery to the police. Detective Williams believes you were there."

‘‘But that’s not true.’’

‘‘He’s calling it premeditated murder. In this state, that buys life.’’

Sunni knew exactly what it bought. And, yes, she was in serious trouble. But at least Joey’s alibi story had given her some breathing room until the police turned over more evidence, evidence that would prove she was innocent.

‘‘I didn’t kill Milo Tandi.’’

‘‘I believe you. But then I’m not the one you need to convince. Williams is sure that, like the scarves, the silk lingerie found in Milo’s apartment is yours.’’

‘‘Milo Tandi ran an escort service out of that apartment. His name is on several other apartments at the Crown Plaza for that same purpose. That lingerie isn’t mine.’’

‘‘Before I arrived at police headquarters did you tell Williams anything I should know about?’’

‘‘No. Only that I didn’t kill Milo, and I wanted my lawyer if they had plans to formally charge me. That’s when you showed up.’’

Smiling, he asked, ‘‘How does Caponelli’s sound?’’

Sunni had never been to the quaint Italian restaurant in Little Italy. She’d heard it was one of the best in the city, but she had no wish to dine out with Joey Masado.

‘‘Did I mention I saw Williams outside on my way in? It looks like he’s giving this case top priority. He’s waiting for one of us to make a wrong move. I don’t make wrong moves, Sunni, and you can’t afford to. Can you?’’

No, she couldn’t. Detective Williams wasn’t the only one keeping a close eye on her. Three days ago

Rambo had moved into the neighborhood with an oversize German shepherd. The tall muscle-machine and his sidekick had been *dogging* her every move. She would easily admit that Joey Masado was both intimidating and dangerous, but Rambo looked like he ate nails for breakfast and used his dog for target practice.

She had the best reason in the world to pick up the phone and call her father for help, only she couldn't. Joey Masado thought her father was dead. And she needed him to keep believing it, because if he found out her father was alive and living in New Orleans as the city's police chief she would lose everything.

Yes, she'd lied about who she was when she'd applied for the lease to open Silks. Frank Masado and his two sons were rumored to be linked with the mob. If that was true, they would never have given her permission to open her shop at Masado Towers—not a police chief's daughter.

Joey brushed the silk past his nose, then stood and dropped the scarf on the desk. "I'll pick you up at seven." He turned to leave, then hesitated. "Show a little skin tonight, Sunni. It'll help sell *us* to Williams."

Rambo joined them for dinner. No, he wasn't sharing their table, but he was at Caponelli's not twenty feet away from where Sunni sat at a cozy table for two with Joey Masado.

"How's the veal?"

Caught with her eyes wandering for the third, or possibly the sixteenth time, Sunni scooped up her wineglass and pressed it to her red-painted lips, her attention back to Joey. Everything she'd heard about the restaurant was true—the food was great, the atmosphere intimate, the lighting soft, the music softer.

"Sunni—" Joey motioned to her plate "—how is it?"

She'd eaten only half of what she'd ordered. She was always careful about the kind of food she ate and the amount. Only food wasn't what was on her mind at the moment. She'd lost her appetite the minute she'd spied Rambo. "The veal is excellent, but I'm afraid my appetite is a little off tonight."

Sunni studied Joey Masado. At the Towers he was called the *money man.* He wore European suits and shoes so shiny they could double as traveling mirrors. She didn't know much about the Masado men, but Frank looked as intimidating as he was handsome. Joey must have taken after his mother. He was softer in appearance, kinder and actually smiled—not often, but at least he knew how.

Tomas Masado, on the other hand—Joey's little brother—was Frank with a chip on his shoulder. As handsome as Joey, he wore his street clothes tight, his vivid scars openly, and his attitude a foot out in front of him.

"I love this place." Joey sampled his wine, savored it, then set the stemmed glass down. "I grew up a few blocks from here. For me this place was always a piece of heaven in the middle of hell."

When they had arrived at the restaurant an attractive elderly woman had rushed forward to greet them. She was small, Sicilian and had offered Joey a motherly hug. After kissing him first on one cheek and then the other, the woman—obviously the owner of Caponelli's—had showed them to their table.

Sunni had followed her progress as the woman had

headed toward the kitchen, but instead of going inside, she'd stopped short and seated herself across from Rambo.

It was a good thing Sunni had been sitting down when she'd spied *him* or she would have melted into the floorboards. At that moment her throat had dried up, and forty minutes later she was still having trouble swallowing.

It was as if she'd been dropped smack into the middle of a gangster movie—she was having dinner with a Wise Guy in a restaurant likely owned by Mama Big Guns who knew Rambo personally.

It couldn't get much worse, Sunni thought, then amended that thought. Over the past few days she had thought long and hard about who this rough-looking muscle-machine might be. Vito Tandi's hired avenger seemed the most likely. That being entirely possible, she had loaded her .22 automatic and had been sleeping with it under her pillow.

The image of this man—whoever he was—aiming a gun at her head sent Sunni's gaze over her shoulder once more. As if Rambo came equipped with internal radar, he glanced up and their eyes locked.

In the movies assassins were usually cold-eyed introverts with nasty acne and bad teeth. But Rambo wasn't the least bit repulsive to look at. Of course, he still could have bad teeth. The words *drop-dead-gorgeous* came to mind. *Dead*...yes, that was the appropriate word to use in the same sentence with an assassin. And with *her,* if she was in fact, his target.

Sunni had all she could do not to leap to her feet and race for the door when Rambo stood and headed toward their table. Heart racing, she watched his long stride eat up the distance while he munched on a piece of garlic bread.

Suddenly it was too late to leap up and go anywhere—he was beside the table. And she was silently choking on her fear.

"You're looking good, Joe. I guess crime still pays."

Sunni's first thought was, no, his teeth are stickpin straight and as sparkling white as pearls. And as for pitted skin—nothing unwanted lined his cheekbones but sun-bronzed smooth skin. Actually, his complexion was a grade or two above average. The second thought she had was that Joey Masado should be offended by Rambo's brazen comment. But instead, he grinned, then added a bit of fuel of his own. "I see you're still breathing. That's amazing for a man in your line of work, Jacky. At least I have bodyguards watching my back. Still carry that Diamondback?"

"And the Hibben."

That piece of information opened up Joey's smile and made Sunni's fear triple. Growing up with a father in law enforcement had taught her more about guns and knives than she'd cared to know. If Rambo carried a Diamondback .38 in his back pocket, and a wicked knife in the other, he was a serious man of action, and she was dead.

While Rambo popped the last of his bread into his mouth, then settled his long-fingered hands on his lean hips, Sunni began to envision how he would *do it.* Strangulation was quick. Then, too, maybe he didn't like things quick. Was torture more his style? Did he like things messy? Bloody? Would he use the Hibben? The Diamondback .38?

"You going to introduce me to your pretty lady, Joe?"

His heavy-hitter voice sent a landslide of chills racing the length of Sunni's spine. She lifted her gaze to his face, still struggling to exist on no air—her lungs had collapsed. Rambo's eyes were a vivid shade of green, but not the least bit empty or cruel like she'd expected. On the contrary, they were a combination of old wisdom and real-life experience.

Sunni did a quick once-over from head to toe without moving a muscle. He wasn't wearing a belt and his faded jeans rode low on his hips. His body appeared to be hell-raiser hard—his flat stomach accentuated by the fact that his stark-white shirt clung to his chest and disappeared into his jeans as if he were one smooth column of steel.

"This is Sunita Blais. Sunni to her close friends." Joey reached out and covered her hand with his, claiming her as if she were something he'd bought and paid for months ago. "Sunni, this is an old friend of mine. Jackson's mama owns this place."

His mother owned the restaurant?

Sunni caught Rambo's gaze linger a moment on Joey's hand covering hers, then his interest shifted to the low bodice of her red V-neck silk shift. He took his time sizing up her cleavage. It was on purpose, she decided. A reminder that he'd already *seen* her—seen her very close to naked standing in front of her bedroom window.

"You look familiar...Sunni." He finally pulled his gaze off her chest to study her face. "Have we met somewhere?"

He knew damn well they hadn't officially met, and yet they had in an unorthodox way she would just as soon forget. She wanted to tell him just what she thought of a man who would feast his eyes on an unsuspecting woman who was in the middle of changing her clothes, but somehow chastising the man who had been following her for the past three days, and quite possibly had been sent to kill her, seemed almost funny.

"Sunni?"

"Hah..." She blinked at the sound of Joey's voice. It was then that she realized she'd been caught musing, that Joey was squeezing her hand, and both men were staring at her waiting for her response. She cleared her throat, sure her face matched the color of her red dress. "No, we've never met."

A private, just-for-her twinkle entered his eyes, and another avalanche of chills washed over Sunni's entire body.

"What kind of business are you in, Sunni? Anything I would be interested in?"

He was toying with her. He'd followed her to work, he'd watched her buy groceries. He knew where she banked. And as far as being interested in her *business*... Men, no matter how diverse their professions, were always interested in what a woman took off last.

Yes, Silks sold feel-good fantasy on a hanger. She hadn't thought about it in quite that way when she'd opened the doors a few years ago, but it was a necessary marketing tool in the competitive world of retail.

Her private musing had again created dead silence. Luckily, like before, Joey came to the rescue. "Sunni owns an exclusive silk shop at Masado Towers. You'll have to check it out when you come by to see me. You're coming, right?"

"Yeah, tomorrow. I just got into town."

That was a lie. He'd been following her for three days.

Rambo eyed her half-eaten plate of food. "Didn't like your veal pizzaiola, Miss Blais?"

Nothing about this man should surprise her. But taking notice of what she'd ordered was unexpected. Again she faltered for words, and again, Joey came to her rescue. "Tell Vina the food was as good as ever."

"I'll tell her."

Joey let go of her hand and reached for his half-full wineglass. "Tomorrow, *mio fratello,* I'll give you a tour and we'll catch up."

Joey had just called Rambo his brother. Knowing that wasn't true in the literal sense, she decided that he was definitely connected in some way to the mob.

He started to turn away, then stopped, his eyes fastening on Sunni's cleavage…then on her face. Grinning, he said, "It's been a pleasure *seeing* you. I look forward to next time."

Dangerous or not—this man needed to know she wasn't going to go down easy. And he needed to know there was more beneath her red silk dress than a memorable set of bubbles. She also had long legs that could run a six-minute mile. And she was no slouch on the firing range with her .22 automatic.

Chin raised, Sunni corrected him. "You mean *meeting* me, don't you…Jackson?"

Undaunted by her challenge, his grin opened up. "That, too, Sunni."

"What was that?" Jackson's mother asked the minute he returned to his chair.

"What was what, Ma?"

"You were flirting with Joey's girlfriend. Instead of ogling his lady, you should be pleased that he's dating again and looking so happy."

"Don't you mean still alive and breathing, Ma?"

Lavina's scowl sent her glasses to the end of her nose. "Jackson, your nasty side is showing again."

He reached across the table and shoved his mother's glasses back up. "Joe's doing what he does best, Ma. What all the Masados do best. I accepted that a long time ago, but that doesn't mean I have to like it."

"I admit I worry about those two boys."

"Joe's got bodyguards watching his back. Lucky doesn't need any. Don't lose sleep over it, Ma."

"What both of those boys need is their best friend showing them a little more compassion."

"They need more than that, Ma. They need Frank shipped off to another planet so they can breathe some fresh air."

Lavina Ward reached out and patted her son's hand. "Joey looked good, though, didn't he? So handsome in that shiny suit. Why don't you get yourself a suit like that?"

"Because I don't have two grand to blow, Ma."

"That suit cost that much?"

"He's Frank's money machine, Ma. Remember?"

"What he is, Jackson, is your best friend."

Yes, he and Joe were friends. Lucky, too. They had formed the Brotherhood when they had been three small boys with no last names, just watching cartoons and playing in his ma's backyard. But then the boys grew into men. Frank put Joe in an expensive suit and

Lucky on the street with a gun in his hand, and everything after that had gotten complicated.

Jackson still didn't understand it, and he knew he probably never would. He was a cop and they were syndicate connected. And still they were his…*fratelli.*

He nodded to Joe as his friend escorted Sunni Blais out of the restaurant, half listening to his mother.

"I said, I wonder what happened between Joey and Sophia D'Lano. They were engaged for over a year, and then he just up and broke it off."

"I heard Frank's still trying to put it back together."

"See, I knew you were keeping track of things back home."

His mother's smile was smug as a bug. "Okay, Ma, so I've kept an eye on Joe and Lucky from a distance. What of it?"

"Nothing. It's just nice to hear, is all."

Jackson leaned back and studied his mother. Her black hair had turned gray and she was sporting a few more age lines around her soft brown eyes. Still, she was a pretty woman for fifty-seven. Best of all, she looked happy. He supposed he owed that to Charlie. The retired military man had moved in across the street five years ago, and had been trying to attract his mother's attention from day one. Recently, in their weekly phone conversations, she'd mentioned him with more frequency.

Attaboy, Charlie, Jackson thought—his mother deserved some happiness. She'd been alone for too many years.

Back on track, he asked, "Do you know Sunni Blais, the woman with Joe tonight?"

"Not before last week. She's the woman the police are investigating in the Tandi murder."

"Did she do it?" Jackson watched his mother's reaction to the question.

"How should I know?"

"There're rumors moving through here daily, Ma. You have to have heard something."

"You can't believe rumors, you know that. But after seeing her..."

"Go on."

"She owns an underwear shop at Masado Towers, Jackson. You're the man who moved to the sin capital of the world. I shouldn't have to tell you that a woman as beautiful as that most likely wears the hundred-dollar underwear she sells. And that kind of expensive silk, dear boy, is made to be seen, not kept undercover." Suddenly eyeing her son's head, she said, "You've cut your hair. What prompted that?"

"The heat." It wasn't a lie. Still, he wouldn't mention he was having boss trouble or she'd start pestering him about moving back to Chicago where he belonged.

She sat back and crossed her arms over her chest to study her son. "It looks good. You look like your father."

It was still hard to talk about his father's death and the dark years prior to it. His father's diabetes had been a nightmare for all of them. "How's the knee, Ma?"

"Like new." She swung her leg out from under the table to show him how easily her knee could move without pain.

When she'd had surgery a year ago, Jackson had returned to Chicago for a week. That had been the one and only time he'd been back since he'd relocated to New Orleans.

"Tell me about your partner."

Jackson hadn't mentioned Mac to his mother, outside the fact that he had a new partner. She still didn't know he was a dog. "Mac made the trip with me."

"Then this is a field assignment, not a vacation?"

"I guess you could call it that."

"You guess? Either it is or it isn't, Jackson."

"Okay, Ma, it's work related." His mother was studying him with one raised eyebrow. "What?"

"This assignment, can you talk about it?"

"It has to do with the Tandi murder, Ma. But that's not for public discussion, okay?"

"You know I never talk to anyone about your work."

He knew that, and that's why he always felt free to bounce ideas off her. "Okay, here it is. Sunni Blais is my boss's daughter. I'm here to clear her name."

His mother's eyes widened with surprise. "That woman is your boss's daughter?"

"What about the old scandal, Ma? Could Milo's death have something to do with the old feud with Frank Masado?"

"It's true the scandal has never really died out. People still talk, still speculate where Grace is buried. But the rules Vito and Frank play by have never changed. It seems more likely that this woman killed Milo. The evidence is pretty convincing."

"But she's innocent, Ma."

"A few minutes ago you asked me what I've been hearing, like your mind wasn't made up. Now you say she's innocent." Lavina shook her head. "I can tell you this much, she doesn't look like a victim."

Mouth-watering curves outlined in red silk flashed behind Jackson's eyes. No, he decided, a woman showing off smother-me-please breasts to the degree Sunni had tonight didn't look like a victim. But did being beautiful and owning a million-dollar chest make her a murderess?

"Women who look like that are dangerous, Jackson. Look what happened to Frank Masado. Grace Tandi was the most beautiful woman alive. Frank knew better than to sleep with his best friend's wife, so why did he? I'll tell you why. Because Grace tricked him into thinking with his Johnson instead of his head."

Jackson grinned. "His what, Ma?"

"You know what I'm talking about." She scowled when Jackson chuckled. "Maybe you should warn Joey to be careful. And take a little of that advice for yourself."

Jackson snorted. "Warn Joe? Like he would listen to me any more than Lucky would."

"You underestimate yourself, Jackson. I can still picture you boys lined up on the couch in the living room watching cartoons. You three used to belly-laugh together so hard that you would turn blue and almost stop breathing. You camped together. Went to movies. Shared spaghetti off the same plate. Slept out in the rain together in that old leaky clubhouse in the backyard. Those two boys had a hand in shaping you, and making you who you are today. And contrary to popular belief, it wasn't Frank who made Joey and Lucky who they are. Who they really are, anyway." Lavina patted her son's arm, then pushed his coffee cup toward him and raised hers in a salute. "Friends forever, Jackson. To the end and beyond."

Jackson raised his cup, then downed the strong coffee and stood. He'd left Mac asleep on the couch, and more than likely something in the apartment needed rescuing by now—the desk chair, the bedspread...his T-shirt. ''So if I get a chance to pick you up a pair of underwear at Silks in the next day or two, what color do you fancy, Ma? Widow-spider black, or chili-pepper, too-hot-to-handle red?''

Lavina took a wild swing at her son and missed. ''What would a woman my age do with silk drawers?''

Jackson leaned down and kissed his mother's cheek, then whispered, ''Give Charlie a thrill. It's his birthday next month, right?'' As he headed for the door, he tossed over his shoulder, ''Maybe a better present would be saying *yes* next time he asks you to marry him.''

Chapter 3

A strange feeling raised the hair on the back of Sunni's neck. It was as if she and Joey had chased a thief out the back door as they had come through the front door.

But that was impossible. She was just spooked, is all. And the blame rested squarely on Rambo's broad shoulders—that wicked grin he'd flashed her a second before he'd walked away from their table had gotten her so flustered her imagination was playing tricks on her.

Sunni shoved the green-eyed demon from her thoughts and concentrated on getting Joey Masado out of her apartment as soon as possible. She said, "You wanted to talk privately. So talk."

"Who's your decorator?"

She glanced toward her dinner date and found him standing in the middle of her living room studying her taste in decor. "Me." As a good host, she was forced to ask, "Would you care for something to drink? Beer? Wine? Something stronger?"

"Beer would be fine. I like all the color."

The Crown Plaza was an upscale apartment complex, but the sterility of white walls and white carpets had driven Sunni on a quest to bring a touch of warmth into her home. She loved bold colors, especially red, and had painted the living room raspberry red, and her kitchen and small dining room, a shade lighter.

A sculptured glass coffee table separated a pair of mustard-yellow leather sofas. Wing chairs in raspberry-and-green-rose-patterned tapestry were used as accents. A number of expensive Tiffany lamps also expressed Sunni's love for color—her favorite a one-of-a-kind Calafar with a giant red-and-amber shade that stood behind one of the sofas. A built-in bookshelf hinted that Sunni's interest in roses was more than just casual—her book collection was as extensive as the fragrant collection she had in her greenhouse.

A dozen damask and silk pillows scattered throughout the living room gave the space a female-shrine feeling, as did the bone china in her kitchen cupboards, and the fresh-cut roses in colorful vases that could be found in every room—even the bathroom.

"Maybe I should have you make a few suggestions for brightening up my suite at Masado Towers."

He turned and Sunni was surprised to find him smiling. The spare expression softened his dramatic good looks and made him appear more human. She rounded the island counter and took one step up to enter the kitchen. As she retrieved the requested beer, she said, "I'm sure you can find someone far more qualified."

Beer in hand, she turned around, knowing that he had followed her into the kitchen. She handed him the beverage, avoiding his warm brown eyes, and headed back into the living room.

"Are you afraid of me?"

She would be a fool to admit it, but she wouldn't lie. Sunni leveled him a look from behind one of the leather sofas. "You said you had something to discuss with me."

"First let me say that I'm not here to force myself on you. So relax. You're beautiful, and I'm sure a night in your bed would be memorable, but I never mix business with pleasure. Tonight is business."

Sunni raised her chin. "Then state your business."

"I know about the deal Milo proposed to you several weeks ago."

He knew about the partnership. How?

Suddenly the room felt too warm. Sunni rounded the sofa and headed for the sliding glass door. She brushed aside the sheer curtain to unlock it, but it was already open. Momentarily surprised, she reminded herself of the fresh roses she'd cut that morning in the greenhouse. She must have forgotten to relock it...again.

"Tomas knew the day Milo approached you. Was that all he wanted from you, just the silent partnership?"

The fall breeze lifted the curtain's hem as Sunni stood gazing at the dark sky. "Milo Tandi's deal included some perks, as he called them. But his image of himself, at least in my book, was terribly overrated.

"Unlike me, Milo liked to mix business with pleasure."

"He didn't hide the fact that he was interested in me personally, but his interest in the partnership was what we talked about. I told him I wasn't interested." Sunni turned to face him. "Why are you still smiling? I thought you would be angry."

"I'm smiling because seeing Milo's expression when you told him no would have been worth a cool million. He doesn't get told no that often."

"True, he didn't like hearing it. That's why he kept the offer on the table."

"Meaning he pressured you?"

"He died before it came to that. But, yes, I think he would have gotten heavy-handed eventually."

"Would he have been successful...eventually?"

"I've sacrificed a lot to make Silks a success. It's mine. I created it, and I should be the one to own it. Completely."

His smile widened. "Very good answer, Sunni. Now, I'm told you have a greenhouse on your terrace. Will you show it to me?"

"You like roses?"

"Is that hard to believe?"

"Honestly?"

"I would appreciate it."

"Yes. You don't look like the flowery type."

His sudden laugh was rich and open. It brought a hint of boyish charm to him that Sunni found attractive.

Inside the greenhouse, she showed him the climbing William Baffins and Celsianas. The long blooming rugosas. England's impressive white Yorks and red Lancasters were some of the most fragrant.

"You did good tonight." Joey leaned across the long work table to take a delicate white Rosa soulieana into his hand and sniff. "If we keep the game going, Williams will back off. These smell like heaven, Sunni." He turned and guided her onto the terrace. In one corner an iron table and two chairs attracted him and he sat.

Sunni remained standing. She said, "I'm confused why you would care one way or the other whether I'm a suspect in the Tandi murder."

"It's important to Masado Towers' image. Don't get me wrong. I believe you're innocent. But a full-scale investigation would be awkward for us. I supplied the alibi as added insurance until Williams wakes up and starts looking in a different direction."

It made sense. An intense investigation for a family connected with the organization could pose serious problems.

She regretted wearing the revealing red shift. She could feel Joey dissecting her again and she turned away, her gaze locking on the fourth floor apartment across the alley. The room was dark at the Wilchard. Was Rambo there, sitting in the dark watching them, or was he still out?

"Did you hear what I said?"

No, she hadn't. Sunni turned. "What?"

"I asked if you were afraid to stay here alone."

She came forward and pulled the chair away from the table and sat across from him. "Should I be?"

"Vito Tandi will be hunting for Milo's killer, as will the police. I could put you up at Masado Towers if you like."

"But I'm innocent, remember?"

"Innocent, but alone. On your lease you didn't list

any sisters or brothers. And with both of your parents deceased, there's no one to protect you."

Sunni nodded, even now determined to keep the lie her secret. It was true what she had told him a short time ago. She had worked too hard to turn Silks into a success. "I'm fine, really."

"I can protect you, Sunni. You can trust that."

His declaration prompted her to question whether or not she should tell him about Rambo. But if they were friends, maybe he already knew that his *fratello* was staying at the Wilchard. No, Rambo had lied. He'd told Joey he'd just gotten into town, which meant he no longer lived in Chicago.

He drained his beer quickly, set the bottle on the table, then stood. "I'm good at what I do, Sunni. But you're going to have to do your part, too."

"My part? I don't understand."

He reached out and pulled her to her feet and kissed her. Kissed her quickly, like a man who had the capability to be as tender as he could be cruel.

As Sunni tried to shove him away, he slid his strong hand up her back and crushed her full breasts against him. He nuzzled her neck, whispered, "Someone's watching us. A shadow at the apartment window across the alley. No, don't look. It's show time, Sunni. Kiss your alibi like a woman in love."

Jackson backed away from the window, but not before the image of Sunni wrapped in Joey's arms revisited him. He had to admit that the kiss he'd just witnessed could have started wet paper on fire.

Clide was going to chew both their heads off, he thought. Sunni's for sleeping behind enemy lines, and his for being the elected sucker to confirm the ugly fact to his boss.

At least Clide would be happy to hear that Sunni hadn't made his suspect list. In four days' time he had narrowed Milo's killer down to a list of four possibilities. The bad news was Frank Masado had made the list. Which meant that if he'd moved on Milo, it would have been Lucky who would have made the hit.

Aware of how little time he had to solve the case, Jackson turned on the floor lamp next to the old desk. Like always, he'd easily become obsessed with the case. But, he admitted, this time was worse. He knew the people involved, and a few of those people were important to him. If it took all night, he was determined to narrow down the suspect list to two instead of four.

Resigned, he peeled off his T-shirt and tossed it on the bed. Mac opened one eye, spied Jackson's shirt a foot from his nose, and with the skill of a master sneak, he slid his paw forward and pulled his partner's only hole-free T-shirt toward him. A few well-placed nudges, and the cotton lump became a pillow for his wide scarred head.

Jackson eyed his partner, then glanced at the jeans he had left on the chair before leaving to have supper with his mother. The jeans were now on the floor, and one ass-end pocket was missing.

Shaking his head, he went to work. An hour later, distracted by Mac's whining, he looked over his shoulder to see the K-9 struggling in sleep—trapped in an obvious nightmare he couldn't forget.

The facts were that Mac had lost Nate two years ago, and Jackson had lost Tom a little over three.

They had nothing in common, save the sudden and tragic loss of their partners, and yet that was the cement that had kept Jackson from returning Mac to the pound five weeks ago—that, and the fact that the canine was on the *List*.

Mac rolled onto his side, still whining and twitching. It was then that Jackson saw *it*, a flash of red.

"What's that, Mac?"

At the sound of his name, the dog jerked awake.

On his feet, Jackson moved to the bed, his hand reaching out to uncover the mystery. But Mac wasn't feeling too obliging. Guarding his treasure, he growled low in his throat.

"Take it easy," Jackson warned.

When Mac relented and turned his head away in resigned submission, Jackson sent his hand beneath the dog's furry coat. When his fingers locked around the silky red strip, he pulled, and the mystery literally sprang forward, snapping Jackson in the chest. "What the hell… So this is why you didn't give a damn about going outside to take a leak when I got home."

Jackson was addressing Mac, but his gaze was locked on the sexy red bra that dangled from his fingertips—a bra that looked surprisingly familiar.

It wasn't hard to figure out where Mac had gotten his loot. The Crown Plaza had a similar fire escape. It would have taken Mac less than five minutes to leave the Wilchard by way of the window, cross the alley and get on Sunni's terrace.

Jackson turned and stared out the window. The case files concerning Mac had ranked him as the number-one dog in the precinct's K-9 unit. If a door or window wasn't locked, he was in…*or out,* whichever the case may be.

He was still staring out the window, still balancing Sunni's bra on the end of his index finger, when his cell phone rang. He snatched it off the desk and jammed it to his ear. "Yeah?"

"Ward?"

Clide. "Chief, how's it going?"

"That's my line, Ward. I thought I told you to stay in touch. What that means is I want to be kept abreast of everything that's going on."

No, he didn't, Jackson thought as he brought the sexy bra to his nose and inhaled deeply. It was hers, all right—there was no doubt. He would never forget how wonderful Sunni Blais had smelled as he stood downwind of her at the restaurant. He had never smelled anything better in his life, and he had always thought that nothing could top the mix of delicious smells coming from Caponelli's kitchen.

"So tell me what you got so far. Anything we can sink our teeth into?"

Jackson ran his tongue over his front teeth, his imagination playing with the idea.

"Ward? I said, what evidence have you uncovered? Give me something that'll make me rest easier tonight?"

Jackson thought a minute. "I got a suspect list."

"Hell, that's good news. How's Sunni? Keeping a close eye on her? What's she been up to tonight."

Jackson moved the expensive piece of lingerie through his fingers. "Ah, she's…home."

"Safe and sound. Good. Good work, Ward."

Jackson tucked a delicate red strap into the waistband of his jeans, then rifled through the papers on the desk. "You suppose if I sent you a couple of names you could run a check on them?"

"That's a damn fine idea, Ward. I'll convince the doc I need my computer. I'll have Ry bring it in. E-mail me the names and I'll have him do the legwork for us."

"I'll do that."

"Keep up the good work, Ward, and remember...whatever it takes to get Sunni in the clear, do it. You got my blessing to raise a little hell."

When Clide disconnected, Jackson tossed the phone on the bed beside Mac, then sauntered to the window. Sunni and Joe were no longer on the terrace, and the living room was dark. A dim light shone through the bedroom curtain.

The possibility that Joe was there spending the night in Sunni's bed bothered him more than it should. But then any man with half a brain would want to be in Joe's shoes, or out of them as the case may be.

For the next hour Jackson stood in front of the window and chain-smoked like a drunk on a bender. Then, just when he had convinced himself he needed to go back to work, a shadow appeared behind the curtain. For a long minute it stood there unmoving, then the curtain was swept back to reveal Sunni in a pale blue robe silhouetted against her dimly lit bedroom.

She knew he was there. Her focus went straight to the Wilchard's fourth-floor window. Their gazes locked, minutes dragged by. Jackson wondered what she was thinking as she stood there like a statue.

He lit a cigarette.

More minutes.

Then she stepped back and let the curtain drop.

Her light went out seconds later, but Jackson didn't

move. He lit another cigarette. Two more cigarettes came and went.

Conceding that he was up for the rest of the night—*up,* as in straight as an arrow and stone hard—he went back to work with Sunni's bra still tucked into his waistband, wishing he had taken the time to figure out how to fix the plumbing.

Chapter 4

Sunni knew she should have called her father, explained the mess she was in, then asked for help. It would have been the most reasonable and the most responsible thing to do. And she would have done just that if she hadn't been so sure that she'd lose her lease for Silks and be tossed out of Masado Towers on her ear.

And after that, Joey would have no reason one way or the other to continue to be her alibi. She wouldn't only be out of business, she'd be in jail.

It had been such a small lie. Well, not that small...but harmless. She'd just wanted Silks to have the best location possible in the city, and Masado Towers was simply the best.

Sunni was in the kitchen still dissecting her grim situation when a knock sounded at the front door. She glanced at her blue silk robe, debating whether she should make a quick change or pretend she wasn't home. The second knock forced her to the door to investigate. She leaned into the door, closed one eye and focused the other on the peephole.

"Omigod… I'm dead."

Sunni's life—past and future—flashed before her eyes. She pressed her hand to her throat, tried to swallow.

Another knock.

"He's finally made his move," she whispered, choking on the words. Would they talk first? she wondered. Or would he just kill her…quick? Or maybe not so quick.

The idea of being dead, no matter how Rambo achieved it, sent Sunni scrambling into her bedroom. Throwing one of her fluffy pillows to the floor, she snatched up her loaded .22—if she was going to die, she wouldn't go down without a fight, she decided.

Sunni emerged from the bedroom with the .22 automatic gripped in her hand, just as she heard Rambo call out, "Sis, you there?"

Sis…

"Come on, Sis. Open up. It's me."

She knew who it was, and her neighbor no doubt did, too—his voice was loud as a bell. Sunni looked out the peephole once more. "Not too smart, Rambo. A man bent on murder doesn't want witnesses."

Witnesses…

Of course, that was it. What she needed was a witness. Before Sunni could second-guess her genius idea, she slid the .22 into her robe pocket and unlocked the door. Please, Edna, be nosy today, she silently prayed, then flung the door wide and bolted through it.

In a flash of blue silk, she was past Rambo. Another second and she was pounding on Edna's door. "Edna! Edna!"

In a jiffy the elderly woman in 404 swung her door open. "Yes, dear?"

"Look at this man, Edna." Sunni spun on her heels and jabbed the air with a nervous finger in the direction of her early-morning caller. "Take a good look, Edna. If you read in the *Tribune* tomorrow that I was found in my apartment with my throat slit, call the police and give them this man's description. Green eyes, Edna. Dark hair, almost black. He hasn't shaved in days."

"Five, to be exact," Rambo supplied. "That's if you want to count today."

Edna angled her head and squinted Jackson Ward into focus. "He looks tall, dear. How tall did you say?"

"Very tall, Edna. He must be—"

"Six three."

"Three, Edna. He said he's six thr—" Sunni snapped her mouth shut and glanced back to find Rambo leaning comfortably against her doorjamb. He was wearing jeans and a brown leather jacket along with an amused smile that didn't exactly make him look nasty or dangerous. Or much like a hit man.

"Handsome? Is he a looker, Sunni? His voice is sure nice."

Edna's question went unanswered, but not for long. Suddenly she shuffled forward in her pink terry-towel bathrobe, fuzzy pink bunny slippers and pink sponge rollers—nine, to be exact. She was three feet from Rambo when Sunni rushed forward and jerked Edna to a stop. "Wait. What are you doing?"

"Getting a closer look, dear." Edna stretched her birdlike neck and licked her crooked lips as she dissected Rambo as if he were the dessert special for Thursday night bingo. Finally, she asked, "Who is he, again?" To Sunni's surprise, Rambo shoved away from the doorjamb and stuck out his hand to her elderly neighbor. "Hi, Edna. I'm Jackson, Sunni's older brother. The one she never talks about."

"Brother? No, I don't believe she mentioned you."

"I'm not surprised. I'm the black sheep in the family."

When Edna reached for his hand, Sunni's jaw dropped. "You are not—"

One minute Rambo was shaking Edna's hand, and the next minute he had successfully captured Sunni around the waist. A quick jerk forward and her body collided with a slab of iron. A solid squeeze after that—using only one arm around her waist—he lifted her off her feet. "God, it's good to see you, Sis."

Another hard squeeze successfully stripped the air from her lungs, and she fought to speak. As she sucked in air, his male scent rushed up to greet her—that and the smell of sweet tobacco and mint toothpaste.

"I should have called first," he told her. "Forgive me, Sis? Please?"

The question wasn't meant to be answered. He followed it up with a fast kiss planted square on her open mouth. Startled, Sunni jerked her head back only to hear him swear softly, then he thrust his free hand to the back of her head and forced her mouth to meet his once more. Their eyes locked in a battle of wills, he whispered, "Be nice," then clamped his shiny white teeth around her lower lip and hung on.

Behind them, Edna said, "Oh, dear, would you look at the time. I had no idea it was so late. *Jeopardy* starts in three minutes. I hope I can move that fast."

Flattened against Rambo, dangling a foot off the floor with her lip caught between his teeth, Sunni heard Edna's famous slipper-shuffle start back to her apartment. Desperate to keep the elderly woman in the hall, she jerked her head back, only to wince in pain when sharp teeth clamped down hard to keep her silent.

Edna's retreating shuffle stopped. "You two have a nice family reunion." Then the sound of her door closing resigned Sunni to whatever fate Rambo had planned for her.

She squeezed her eyes shut as he stepped inside her apartment and closed the door. Sunni felt his arm loosen up around her waist enough to allow air to filter back into her lungs. Eyes still closed, her lip still caught between his teeth, her heart beat like an African drum in her chest.

A minute must have elapsed before he released her lip. Afraid to open her eyes, Sunni opted to keep them closed. That is, until something warm and wet slid over her lower lip. The unexpected sensation brought her eyes open in one quick blink.

"You're bleeding."

Her tongue went to investigate, and sure enough, she tasted blood. "What's next?"

"Next?"

"A quick kill, or are you one of those sadistic animals who enjoys seeing his victim beg?"

It appeared he was struggling to keep from smiling. A warning bell sounded in Sunni's head.

"Begging is good in some instances. But in this case, I think you've got me confused with somebody else, Sis. I'm here to keep you from being a victim, not make you into one."

"Who are you?" Sunni insisted.

"You know who I am. We met last night."

"Okay, then *what* are you?"

"I've never liked the word *bodyguard,* but if that word works for you, then—"

"Bodyguard?" Shock cracked Sunni's voice. "You're not connected? A hit man?"

"No."

"Bodyguard? My…bodyguard?"

"That's right.

Relieved yet confused, Sunni demanded, "Put me down."

"First we negotiate."

Sunni narrowed her eyes. "Negotiate what?"

"I need a shower. Agree to let me use yours, and I'll put you down."

"Your apartment is right across the alley. Use your own shower."

"No water. It's your fault, really. If you lived on the second or third floor I wouldn't have bargained with old man Ferguson for the fourth. The Wilchard's plumbing is out on that floor."

The humor in what he was saying took Sunni by surprise. And so did the desire to believe what he was saying.

"You find that funny, Sis?"

"Very. Swear you're not a hit man."

"If I was, you would have been dead four days ago."

There was some truth in that. And last night at the window she'd had the strangest feeling. It was as if he was watching over her. "All right. A shower if you can prove you're who you say you are. Now, put me down."

He set her down, then reached into his pocket. Sunni thought he meant to show her his ID, but when he produced her .22, she nearly fainted. "Oh, God!"

"Take it easy. Silk pockets are lousy for hiding heavy hardware. Noticed it the minute you bolted through the door." He grinned, then studied the .22 in his hand. "Do you know how to shoot this?"

"Yes."

"Can you hit what you're aiming at?"

"Why not hand it over and I'll show you?"

His grin spread, then he sobered and walked over to the island counter and laid down the gun—but not before checking to see that the safety was on. After that, his gaze traveled from Sunni's face to the swell of her breasts. "Just so I have the facts, how long have you been sleeping with Joe?"

His question turned Sunni's cheeks hot. Only, she knew what had prompted the question. Last night he had witnessed her and Joey Masado kissing. And it hadn't been just a friendly kiss. Joey had told her to kiss him like a woman in love.

"Come on, Sis. I know Joe was here last night, and we both know how I know that." Her continued silence had him rubbing his whiskered jaw as he continued to take her apart with his eyes. ''I didn't hear you. Are you or are you not doing the horizontal hustle with him?''

Sunni drew her robe together to lessen the amount of cleavage on display. She wasn't sure if it helped, but she'd be damned if she'd check. ''That question wasn't part of our deal,'' she finally said. ''I won't discuss my personal life with a stranger. At least not until you can prove to me you are who you say.''

He parted his jacket and settled his long-fingered hands on his hips. ''I've seen a lot of you lately, Sis. I don't consider us strangers.''

Sunni knew what he was getting at. She clamped her mouth shut, then winced when renewed pain shot into her bruised lower lip.

''If I'm going to keep you alive, I need to know everything about you. That includes whose bed you frequent and who you've passed your apartment key around to. There was a murder five days ago, and you're the PD's number-one suspect. You forgotten that?''

''No. But I didn't kill Milo Tandi.''

''You have no motive as far as I can tell. But those scarves manacled around the DB's wrists are damn incriminating, Sis. And this time the CSU didn't screw up the evidence when they collected it. Your prints are crystal.''

Another warning bell set off inside Sunni's head. She'd lived with a cop for more than twenty years—her father used cop slang constantly. DB meant *dead body*. CSU was the crime scene unit. Only a cop would use that kind of slang. Only a cop would—

''Are you Joey's window dressing, Sis, or the beautiful woman caught in the middle of an old feud? If you're the woman in the middle, I'll warn you it isn't a healthy place to be sitting right now. Powerful men in powerful places think human life can be bought and sold as easily as real estate. The Masado boys and the Tandis are powerful players in an old organization. You could be taking a swim in concrete if you've been bed hopping."

More words and phrases convinced Sunni that—

The phone rang.

Sunni jumped, then stared at the phone on the island counter just a foot away from where her *bodyguard* stood. On the second ring she started forward.

"Let the machine take it."

She ignored his rusty-nail voice as well as his intimidating stance. As she reached for the phone his hand covered hers and remained there like an iron paperweight.

"I want to hear who it is."

Five rings later the answering machine clicked on. "Sunni, it's Joey. Detective Williams paid me a visit early this morning. He claims he called your father four days ago after being assigned to Tandi's murder investigation. You can imagine my surprise when he told me Clide Blais was your father. Especially since my records say your father and mother are dead and buried in Mississippi. A police chief for the city of New Orleans, is what Williams claims. That explains why Jacky's in town. A few phone calls and I've learned that your father's ace flew in five days ago as the mop crew. What's your scam, Sunni? Ten o'clock in my office."

* * *

"You're a sleazy cop?"

The force of her words nailed Jackson where he stood. "Homicide detective," he corrected her.

"You're a con man with the morals of a snake."

"Bodyguard protecting the boss's daughter."

"Stalker."

"You must have me confused with that other guy," Jackson returned. "The one who was tailing you the day I got here."

Her eyes widened. "Someone's been tailing me, other than you?"

"Not any longer. So Mommy and Daddy are buried in Mississippi, is that the story? That's funny 'cause I just talked to Daddy last night."

"What do you mean by, *not any longer?*"

Jackson was trying to keep his temper corralled, but she was treading close to the end of his patience. She had no idea what he had been doing on her behalf since he'd gotten into town—without running water, no less.

"If I'm going to be any use to you, I'm going to need your cooperation. As far as the stalker goes, he had a record. People who lie and cheat are usually easy to trip up. That leads us back to why Joe's file on you is full of lies."

She glared at him. "I don't cheat. The lie…the lie didn't hurt anyone. About the stalker…"

"Whoever paid him to watch you, paid him enough to keep his mouth shut. I explained to him that if he didn't tell me who that was, he'd be jailed on a charge he couldn't beat. He didn't believe me." Jackson shrugged. "He'll do a year. Now, about this suspect mess—"

"This mess, as you call it, Mr. NOPD, isn't my doing."

"It doesn't matter. It's still in your face, *Sis*. That's what matters. And Stud Williams goes by the book, sweetheart. If you're on his suspect list, he's got a damn good case, and the power to ruin your life."

"So what are you doing about it...*Ace?*"

"I've been turning this city inside out to rescue your cute butt, that's what I've been doing. And at the same time, I've been keeping an eye on you so—"

"I know exactly what you've been keeping an eye on, you snake. And I'm sure my father would be interested to know what kind of man he's sent to *rescue* me."

Jackson tried to keep a straight face, but even when she was angry, chewing tail, he liked looking at her. And that voice...oh, yeah, he definitely liked her husky voice. It didn't fit her petite size, but then neither did the amount of frontage she was carrying. His grin widened.

"That grin is going to cost you, Ace."

He should back off now, but Jackson had never been shy when it came to throwing another log on a hopping good blaze. And that was another lesson she needed to learn if they were going to work together without drawing blood. His gaze went to her swollen lip. "How was I supposed to know you were a practicing exhibitionist, Sis? If I had, I would have steered clear of the window."

"You arrogant, oversize—"

Jackson held up his hand. "Whoa! I'm here to get you out of a tight spot, not to fight with you."

"And why didn't you bother telling me this days ago?" She straightened to her full height and still the top of her head was below Jackson's chin. "I've been sleeping with my gun under my pillow, one eye open and a foot on the floor, thinking you were a hit man for Vito Tandi, you slippery snake."

Jackson stepped into the kitchen and opened the fridge. He hadn't eaten since last night and his stomach was attacking his ribs. "Next time someone comes to the door you don't know—" he reached for the egg carton on the bottom shelf "—don't open it." He straightened and set the eggs on the counter and faced her across the counter. "Bolting into the hall to raise the neighbors wouldn't have saved you if I had come to kill you. Dead is dead, whether you're bleeding in comfort—" he eyed her white plush living room carpet "—or facedown in the hall. The money's the same to a contract killer."

Jackson went in search of a frying pan.

"Why didn't my father call to tell me you were coming?"

"Why didn't you call?"

"I didn't want to worry my parents."

"Or have to explain the lie to Joe once Daddy climbed out of the grave."

"Okay, so maybe that was part of it."

"All of it."

"Okay, yes. If I had called, then Joey Masado would have found out my father is in law enforcement."

"And that's a bad thing?"

"If you were a Masado would you want a cop's daughter leasing space in your building?"

If what she said was true it meant that Sunni Blais wasn't a manipulative bitch. He said, "Masado Towers isn't the only place in the city you could have set up shop."

"Expensive lingerie, like expensive accommodations, aren't a necessity. Both make you feel good, but you can live without them unless there is no reason why you should have to."

"So it was all business? The lie was born to get the lease?"

"They say location is everything. Are you any good?"

Jackson located the pan and set it on her stove. "Are we talking job stats or my charisma?" He wiggled his dark eyebrows as his gaze locked with her sultry gray eyes—bedroom eyes that suited her lush body and husky voice.

"You have no charisma. You kiss like a camel. Of course I'm talking about your ability to clean up my *mess*. The way my luck is going this week, you're no doubt a loser and the only detective my father could get to fly up here on short notice."

"Don't be shy, Sis, tell me how you really feel." Jackson spied the coffeemaker, the glass pot full of coffee. After opening four cupboards and studying a set of bone china cups the size of a doll's tea set, he palmed a toy cup and filled it to the brim. Staring into the tiny cup, he said, "We're going to have to do something about these. I don't want to smell my morning coffee, I want to drink it."

When he turned to face her once more, her pretty

eyes were narrowed, her sexy mouth pinched and emphasizing the damage he'd done to her lower lip. She was right, he'd muddled that kiss. The only explanation he had was that his decision to play loving brother in the hall had backfired. Touching her hadn't been part of the plan and neither had Edna, or the kiss.

"I'm getting dressed."

"Helluva good idea. Shiny-penny perfect," Jackson muttered under his breath, not finding fault, just stating a fact—Sunni Blais would always be the shiniest penny in the pile. He'd pegged her as a perfectionist the moment he laid eyes on her. And the inside of her house verified the fact. It should turn him off cold, but the truth was nothing about Sunni turned him off.

"What did you say?"

"I said, I'll make breakfast. While we eat, we'll talk."

"I don't have time to talk. I'm supposed to meet Joey Masado at ten. I'm going to need time to figure out what I can say to him to convince him not to throw me and Silks to the wolves."

Jackson took one swig of coffee and emptied the silly cup. As he set it on the counter, he said, "From here on out I'm your bodyguard, brother, husband, best friend and priest all wrapped into one. What you're going to say to Joe, Stud Williams, and anyone else who comes along, will be discussed first with me. And don't worry about Joe. I'll smooth things over with him. We're old friends."

Her face suddenly paled. "So, you're one of *those* kind of cops."

Jackson had been accused more than once of being on the take when he worked for the CPD. Yes, there were plenty of dirty cops in the city, but he wasn't interested in labels, just doing the job his conscience told him to do. "I don't play by black-and-white rules. I play by my rules."

"My father's golden boy isn't so golden? Does he know?"

Jackson flashed his sparkling white teeth. "Your father didn't choose me because I fit some golden-boy mold, or because he likes me. I put six cases on hold to fly out the same day he asked me to save Saint Sunni. You see, down-and-dirty is familiar territory for me, Sis. That's who I am, the *whatever-it-takes* cop at the NOPD. My specialty—too hot to handle. Which is lucky for you because my legwork so far has convinced me that this case is going to get a whole lot hotter before it cools down and goes away."

"Well it's not going to cool down and go away now that Joey Masado knows who my father is. He's probably called police headquarters already and recanted his alibi story."

"He can't recant fact."

She said nothing.

"You're saying Joe lied? You have no alibi?"

"Of course he lied. Why would I have dinner with Joey Masado in his suite late at night?"

"I can think of a number of reasons. We still haven't established your relationship with him yet."

Her hands settled on her hips, parting her robe and letting the *twins* breathe. "I'm not Joey's window dressing. We are not doing the horizontal hustle. And I haven't been playing Ping-Pong with the Tandis and the Masados. Climbing into bed with gangsters would be about as smart as taking up sword-swallowing after one night at the circus.''

In animated frustration her hands left her hips to toss her hair out of her eyes. Her robe parted further and Jackson's eyes were drawn to the juggling act going on in the center ring. Enjoying the show, he asked, ''So you've never slept with Joe?''

''Of course not.''

''How about Milo Tandi?''

''No.''

''But you knew him?''

''Since I've lived in the city we talked twice in person, and twice on the phone.''

The conviction in her voice made Jackson believe her, even though it was a proven fact she wasn't above lying. Still, if she wasn't *bedding* anyone, what was that kiss all about on the terrace last night?

''What about Joe's brother? How well do you know Lucky?''

''Lucky?''

''Tomas Masado.'' When they were kids, he and Joe had given Tomas the nickname Nine-lives Lucky because he had used up all his nine lives before he'd reached the age of sixteen.

''I don't know Tomas very well. When we've talked it's always been about business matters. We don't move in the same circles.''

''You said you talked with Milo. Was that the night you went to the Shedd to meet him?''

''I never went to the Shedd to meet him.''

''I have witnesses who put you there a few weeks ago seated at a table with him.''

"I was there, but not to meet him. I went there to meet Elizabeth."

"Elizabeth?"

"Elizabeth Carpenter. She used to work for me. She called and asked if I could bring her last paycheck by the Shedd as a favor. But she never showed up. I was leaving when Milo Tandi appeared at my table and invited himself to sit down. He said he wanted to speak to me about something. He bought me a drink, then started talking about a partnership idea he had for Silks. He wanted to become my silent partner."

"And?"

"And I turned him down. I talked to Joey about this last night. He already knew Milo had approached me. He said Lucky knew it the night he asked me."

"You said you talked to Milo twice on the phone. About the partnership?"

"Yes. He kept sweetening the pot. He offered me a percentage of his escort business profits. I said no."

"And he just accepted that?"

"No, he called again. Then he showed up here, in the lobby. He made his pitch again in the elevator."

"When was that?"

"Three days before he was killed."

"Did anyone see you two together that day?"

"Yes. The front desk manager saw him get in the elevator with me. I assume Detective Williams knows that. He's already talked to everyone who works here."

"Did you and Joe ever date before he showed up at the police station claiming to be your alibi?"

"No."

"So it was just business as usual until Milo was hit."

"Yes."

"At the restaurant you two didn't look like strangers," Jackson pointed out, still having a hard time forgetting what he'd seen.

"He said the alibi story needed to appear real. Detective Williams has been very persistent."

"What about afterward?" Jackson tried to ignore what the question was doing to his insides.

"Afterward?"

"On the terrace last night."

"Joey spotted you. Not you specifically, but a shadow at the window across the alley. The kiss was just for looks to sell the alibi story to whoever was at the window."

"But you knew who was at the window."

"Yes, but Joey didn't."

"And you didn't tell him."

"There really wasn't time. And I didn't know who you were. Who you worked for. Who to trust."

If that kiss had been faked, what was Sunni Blais capable of if she cared about the man she was tasting? The question had Jackson wincing as his imagination turned up the heat inside his already tight jeans.

"Joey Masado is the reason I'm not in jail right now. I don't know him very well, but I am grateful for the alibi."

"Just how grateful were you last night, Sis?" The question could squeak by as being a job-related inquiry, but Jackson's motivation was fueled by something he wasn't very proud of at the moment—a sudden possessiveness that made no sense at all.

"Joey Masado didn't slip out of my bed before dawn, if that's what you're asking. Was that why you were glued to your window last night? Were you actually working, Ace, or do you like to watch?"

He'd always thought of himself as an action man. But lately, watching Sunni Blais had been nothing short of pure pleasure.

"What, no explanation for window shopping at midnight?"

Jackson blinked, irritated that she was picking at an already open sore. "There's something else you need to know about me, Sis. I don't explain or apologize for anything I do. Now, go put some clothes on before you get a chest cold. Breakfast will be ready in twenty minutes."

Chapter 5

For the past two years, Sunni had given herself a measured dose of insulin at exactly six-thirty, then eaten breakfast thirty minutes later. On her way to the closet, she glanced at the crystal clock on her nightstand, knowing exactly why she was feeling shaky and so anxious she could jump out of her skin—breakfast was late by an hour.

"Routine is everything," she whispered, then grabbed a silk suit from her closet and tossed it on the bed. "Stay calm," she added, then mentally began to list why that wasn't going to be possible.

Besides, her stress level was on its way through the roof for reasons having nothing to do with breakfast. Her father had sent Ace to clean up her mess. Joey Masado knew she was a manipulative liar. And Detective Williams was convinced she'd killed Milo Tandi.

Swearing that an evil genie had taken up residence in her house, Sunni stepped into her silver silk skirt, then shot her arms into a matching short-waisted suit jacket before realizing she'd forgotten her bra. "Damn!" Frustrated, she tugged open her drawer, pulled out the first bra she saw—a black lace push-up—and tossed it on, then the suit jacket once more.

As if a tornado had taken control of her hands, she quickly brushed her hair, then tucked and twisted and pinned. When she turned to the mirror to make sure she'd hidden all the pins, her hair was forgotten as her eyes locked on her lip. "Oh, God! I look like Honey Harlot." Her gaze fell to the open vee of her jacket and she cursed the bra she'd literally tossed on. Her breasts looked as if they matched her lower lip—swollen twice their normal size. Peeling off her jacket, she started over.

Minutes later, in the hall, Sunni brushed her fingers over her swollen lower lip, squared her shoulders, then assessed the situation in the kitchen. She was half expecting to see flames shooting out of the toaster—it would certainly top off the morning. But there were no flames, and the heavenly aroma of crispy bacon and onions made her stomach growl. Mr. NOPD actually cooked.

He'd removed his jacket and rolled up his shirt-sleeves. Sunni stared at his hairy forearms, then at his skilled wrist action as he beat a bowl of eggs. He turned to search the counter for something, and that's when she caught sight of her dishcloth jammed into the back pocket of his jeans—the left pocket. The right pocket was missing.

He had a nice butt, she decided—nice definition.

Not too flat. Not too round. No doubt solid and hard like the chest she'd been crushed against in the hall.

He must have sensed her presence. He said, "Three minutes and we can eat."

Their eyes locked briefly before Sunni glanced at the already set table. When she spied the tall glasses of orange juice, she rounded the counter and reached for one of them. Her back to him, she took two unladylike gulps of the sweet juice.

"I hope scrambled is okay. Like onions?"

"Scrambled is good, onions...they're okay." She took another healthy gulp. "Did you learn to cook at Caponelli's?"

"No. My ma worked a lot. If I wanted to eat something besides peanut butter on bread, I had to learn to cook. It was mostly by trial and error."

She turned around ready to say something rude, but when she spied the fluffy scrambled eggs, she forgot what she was going to say—they were so light and airy they looked like yellow cotton candy.

"Margo calls me a hungry woman's fantasy."

The comment sent an unexpected shiver up Sunni's spine. Yes, she knew all about a hungry woman's fantasy. But her late-night dreams never seemed to be about food. The thought sparked the memory of pearly white teeth sinking into her lip, then how hard Ace's granite body had felt.

He held up the eggs. "What do you think?"

Sunni blinked out of her fog, blamed her reckless thoughts on her lack of food and asked, "Who's Margo?"

"She's my ex-partner's wife. She cooks, but not happily. When Ry invites me over, I usually do the cooking. Sit down. I'll bring the eggs.'' Gladly, Sunni thought, and took a chair. He placed the platter of eggs and bacon in the middle of the table, then a stack of toast. Seconds later he covered the chair across from her, his masculine scent greeting her once more.

She eyed the crispy strips, the too-fluffy eggs. She never ate bacon on Monday, but right now she would eat the leg off the chair she was sitting on if she thought it would chase away the dizziness that had suddenly sent her head spinning

The tingling sensation in her lips clinched it, and Sunni touched her swollen lower lip, knowing that she'd just been given another warning that she needed food as quickly as possible.

''Still hurt?''

''What?'' She glanced at him, then snatched up a piece of bacon and munched it down in two bits. ''No. Yes... I mean, yes, a little.''

''You pulled away.''

''You vampired my lip.''

He was in the process of shoving scrambled eggs onto his plate when his hand stilled and he cocked his head and grinned at her. ''Vampired? Is that a word?''

''I don't care if it is or not. It's what you did.'' Sunni took two more strips of bacon and then inhaled a piece of toast. She would have refilled her empty juice glass, but she didn't think she could reach the fridge without falling on her face—her knees felt suddenly weak.

When she focused on him again, he smiled. A sexy smile that showed off his pretty teeth—polished pearls in a sea of dark whiskers. Yes, he had great teeth. Amazing, since he was also a smoker. She knew this because he'd had a cigarette between his lips practically every time she'd seen him over the past four days—except for this morning.

She served herself a mound of eggs. "You didn't have to do it...bite me."

"I didn't plan to." He shrugged, dug his fork into his eggs. "Hi, Sis, long time no see. After a line like that, it seemed natural for a brother to kiss his sister." He looked up. "You're not going to hold it against me, are you? I didn't enjoy it."

She knew damn well why his grin had grown, and exactly what she'd felt sandwiched against his hard body. Unless he owned a pet rock, he'd been more than a little aroused by the time he had set her down inside her apartment.

"Just another dirty job, right? But then you're good with down-and-dirty, ah...Ace? Isn't that what you said?"

"See, you really are as smart as you look."

Sunni patiently waited for the food to chase away the common symptoms of a diabetic off her schedule.

"Like my cooking, do you?"

Sunni looked down at her empty plate, her mouth a little too full to answer without sharing her eggs. She nodded. Swallowed. "Tell me why my father didn't call to tell me you were coming. You never did say."

"After Williams called, and you didn't, he thought something might be wrong. Suddenly coming in waving a flag didn't seem too smart. Not until we knew what we were up against." He popped a piece of bacon into his mouth and chewed. "The other thing you need to know, something your father didn't want me to mention, is that he's been hospitalized. One of his ulcers is acting up."

"He's in the hospital?"

"You knew he had ulcers, right?"

"Yes."

"Then you know it's happened before. It's not too serious, just inconvenient right now. If you want to call him, go ahead. Only I wasn't supposed to tell you he was in the hospital. But I figure you're smart, Sis. Lying seems like a waste of time for both of us. And you're a big girl, right? Dancing around the truth just wastes time."

"You're sure he's all right?"

"In a week or two he'll be back at it. I guarantee it."

Sunni knew her father's ulcer condition was aggravated by stress. She had to ask. "Did his ulcer flare up after Detective Williams called him?"

"I wish I could say no, but it happened a few hours later."

"How long have you worked with my father?"

"Three years."

"But you grew up here?"

"That's right."

"Why did you leave?"

"For a change of scenery."

Sunni didn't know if he was telling the truth this time—he'd set his jaw—but asking too many personal questions could prompt him to do the same. Yes, she'd heard his little sermon about honesty, but she wasn't the confessing type. Feeling stronger, no longer weak or dizzy, she stood and took her dirty plate to the sink.

"It's not a good idea to eat so fast. Bad for the digestive system. And if you're ulcer material like your father, you should watch what you eat."

What was bad was eating over an hour late when your body required a rigid schedule to function like a normal person's. But Sunni wasn't about to surrender her secret. "I'm in a hurry. I don't want to be late for work," she reasoned.

"Does it matter? Mary opens up, anyway. The store runs whether you're there or not."

That he knew her manager's name or Mary's capabilities didn't surprise Sunni. This man had already proved he was resourceful.

"Tell me why Williams is so sure you killed Milo Tandi. What's supposed to be your motive?"

Sunni began to put the kitchen back in order. "Lover's quarrel."

"He thinks you got into an argument after you tied him up?"

"He did present that theory."

"So you two were playing torture-me-please, got into a quarrel in the middle of your sex-fest, and you blew his head off."

His visual description was followed by dead silence. Sunni bent over and started to load the dishwasher. "Another idea Detective Williams came up with was that we quarreled in the elevator three days earlier, and that I went to meet Milo that night intent on killing him. Premeditated murder. He seemed to like that idea best."

"Do you know how your scarves got into that apartment?"

The words were spoken too close. Sunni jerked upright and turned quickly, nearly colliding into his broad chest. Scrambling for something to say, she settled for "More coffee?"

He took a step back and gazed at the empty china cup that looked ridiculously tiny in his big hand, then at the coffeemaker. Then her. "Do you have a straw? Maybe I could suck it out of the pot."

Sunni didn't want to like this man or his dry humor, but she couldn't keep from smiling. "I didn't realize those cups were that small when I bought them."

His eyes swept her body, and as she leaned against the counter, she decided to return the favor. Jackson Ward looked like his Sicilian mother in many ways—his prominent nose, his dark hair, dark complexion. But his electric green eyes didn't fit the mold. He had beautiful teeth. A rugged strong jaw.

Full lips.

Actually, she'd lied about him kissing like a camel—if you could call what they'd shared an actual kiss. His lips had been warm and softer than she'd expected them to be.

The open vee of his shirt guaranteed that his chest was hairy, possibly clear to his waist. He'd eaten left-handed. His nails were clean and trimmed short. He'd used his napkin.

And all this meant what?

"Hey, Sis," he waved his hand in front of her eyes, "I asked you how you think your scarves got into that apartment?"

Back on track, Sunni said, "I can't. My apartment has never been broken into."

"You sure about that?"

"Yes. I would know."

"Would you? You have a lot of...scarves?"

"Yes."

"So a few missing wouldn't be obvious?"

"I suppose not."

"You identified the scarves. Why?"

"Because they were mine. They have my initial on them. They're one-of-a-kinds."

He drained his coffee cup in a single gulp, then shoved away from the counter and turned his cup upside down on the top rack of the dishwasher. "Who would know that?"

Sunni stared at the cup for a couple of seconds. "I don't know."

He cleared the table quickly, then began rinsing the dishes one by one and arranging them in the dishwasher. "Think."

"My employees, I suppose."

"Ever leave your scarves at the store? In your office?"

"Yes, I suppose I have."

"How about your keys to this apartment? Who has one?"

"Edna has a key."

"Only Edna?"

"Yes."

"Do you have an employee file on each of the women who work for you?"

"Yes. But none of them would be capable of stealing."

He stopped to look at her. ''What about Elizabeth Carpenter? You said she worked for you, then quit. Sounds like she might have set you up to meet Milo that night at the Shedd.''

Sunni hadn't thought about that. ''You think so?''

''I'll check her out today.'' He glanced at his watch. ''I should check on Mac, too.''

''Is Mac your dog?''

''My partner.''

''The dog with mange is your partner?''

''Mange?''

''He's missing hair,'' she said, pointing out the obvious.

''Those are battle scars.''

He rinsed out the sink, wiped it down with a paper towel and tossed it in the garbage. He must have taken her kitchen apart while she'd been in her bedroom to know where everything went, she thought.

Suddenly he stepped forward, close enough for Sunni to get another solid whiff of his masculine scent. ''Better put some ice on that.'' He reached up and touched her lower lip, his thumb carefully brushing over the puffy area where his teeth had split the skin. ''Hurt much?''

''It looks worse than it feels,'' she admitted.

He dropped his hand. ''Want to get even? Bite me back?''

Sunni stared at his mouth as if considering his offer. ''And you'd just stand there and take it?''

''I would suffer through it, yeah. I don't say anything I don't mean...Sis. What about you? Can I believe what you say?''

''About what?''

"You promised me the use of your shower. That offer still stand?"

"How long did you say you were without running water?"

"Four days now. Five if we're counting today."

Sunni hesitated, then finally nodded. "Yes, you can use my shower. Down the hall and to your right. Towels are—"

"I'll find them."

Sunni watched him saunter out of her kitchen. A minute later she heard him whistle. Knowing why he had been inclined to do so, she squeezed her eyes shut as she imagined him standing in her bathroom, his eyes assessing the naked lovers etched on her shower door. The phantom-lover idea was a bit over the top—another decorating liberty she'd taken.

The walls in the bathroom she'd left white, opting to use color in the fixtures instead. She'd chosen decadent lavender, and used a deep shade of plum slate for the shower and flooring. The etched glass shower door had been custom made—the naked lovers entwined in a carnal embrace inspired by a private fantasy that kept her company most nights.

She waited, listened for the second whistle. When it came, she knew he'd opened the shower door and found the ceiling mirror.

An odd noise out on the terrace was a welcome distraction, and Sunni left the kitchen and shoved back the curtain in the living room to find Jackson's partner pawing at her door frame. "Stop that," she scolded.

Instead of heeding her warning, the dog began to work faster, his long claws digging deep grooves into the vulnerable wood frame.

"No!" Sunni unlocked the door and shot it open. "I said stop!"

The German shepherd was inside her apartment in one aggressive leap. His next move put him on his hind legs and in Sunni's face. She staggered backward into the bookshelf as the dog planted his paws on her shoulders, then offered her a kiss that sent his long tongue over her face from chin to forehead in one very wet, slippery slurp.

"Nooo..." She shoved the dog down and wiped slobber off the end of her nose and chin. Still leaning against the bookshelf, she watched him bolt across her white carpet and down the hall. Seconds later he was back—his interest focused on the kitchen. She was still against the bookshelf wiping slobber when he stood on his hind legs, put his paws on the island counter and looked across it at her.

She cringed as his sharp dark eyes studied her, then the living room. A vision of him lifting his leg on the edge of one of her sofas made her groan out load. The noise brought his attention back to her, and that's when she noticed he was missing part of one ear. His many scars made him look like a bad boy who had enjoyed earning the title, and as arrogant as his two-legged partner.

Suddenly he made one powerful lunge that easily carried him over the counter and put him in the middle of one of her leather sofas.

"Omigod!" Sunni's jaw dropped, then dropped another inch as he bounced over her glass coffee table to the other sofa without touching the floor. Wagging his tail as if he'd just been given the key to the castle, he jumped over the back of the sofa and nearly took out her eighteen-hundred-dollar Tiffany.

"No!" She made a mad dash to rescue the red-and-amber Calafar. "Jackson!"

The dog jackknifed around and looked at her as if she'd said the magic word. Suddenly he barked, then started spinning in a circle in the middle of the room.

Sunni abandoned the lamp and raced down the hall yelling for Jackson. On reaching the bathroom door, she jerked it open and…

Sunni wanted to move, she really did, but her feet felt as if they'd been nailed to the floor. She didn't hear what Jackson said as he met her gaze. His lips were moving, but the shower spray prevented the words from escaping the erotic glass cage that held him captive. His hand reached for the lavender towel atop the rim of the shower. The shower door opened.

He stepped out of the shower, drawing the towel around his iron-hard belly. "This better be good, Sis, because… What's wrong? You look like someone just aimed a loaded gun at your head."

This man certainly had a way with words, Sunni thought, her gaze tracking several water beads that were on their way down his hairy chest heading south toward his navel.

"Sis…"

"It's Mac. He's… Something's wrong with him. I've got to go now. I'm going now. Work…that's where I'm going now. Late… I can't be late."

Sunni knew she sounded like a robot ready to short-circuit, knew nothing she had said made sense. Retreat was the only thing that would save her now, and she forced her feet to move. In the living room she found Mac still spinning. Only he'd added a piercing bark to his antics as he chased after his tail. He had obviously lost a few brain cells in one of the battles Jackson had referred to earlier—brain cells and fur, along with part of an ear.

She raced out of her apartment and hurried to the elevator, refusing to look back as Jackson called out to her. She poked the button, anxious to escape. The elevator doors opened just as he stepped out of her apartment. Sunni's eyes widened—if Edna was watching, she'd just been granted an eighty-six-year-old woman's fantasy and dying wish all at once—Jackson Ward in a lavender loincloth was one awesome sight.

''Come on back inside, Sis,'' he called out to her. ''Sometimes he acts that way. He's just excited to see you.''

Chapter 6

Masado Towers was definitely a hotel for the rich and famous. The five-hundred-room hotel advertised three restaurants, two lounges, boutiques, swimming pool, and fitness and conference centers. And that was just for starters.

The building had been deep in construction when Jackson had left three years ago. At that time it was hard to tell what it was going to look like. But it looked fabulous—the outside structure, three marble-and-granite towers to add to the Chicago skyline; the inside finished off in Italian marble, old-world murals, rich wood and mansion elegance.

Again, like he had the first day he'd stood inside the gold-plated front doors, Jackson felt a sense of brotherly pride for what Joe had accomplished. Smiling, he gazed at the private glass elevator that climbed more than forty stories, knowing exactly where it led and the idea that had inspired it.

Yes, the hotel was five-star all the way, complete with a lobby surrounded by water gardens, live foliage and polished marble walkways you could see yourself in.

He glanced across the little stone bridge to the elaborate display window where a full-size stuffed lion stood stalking a beautiful female mannequin outfitted in a red silk nightgown. Still smiling, he admitted Sunni Blais, like Joe, sure knew how to make a statement. And an entrance and exit, he mused, remembering the look on her face when she'd raced into the bathroom, then exited a few minutes later just as quickly.

While he stood enjoying the memory, a low growl sounded at his side. He glanced down, saw Mac's eyes lock on Sunni's lion and swore. "Don't even think about it," he warned. "No smart-ass stunts. Got it? As it is you're going to have to work damn hard to get on the good side of Sis after what you pulled this morning. And she doesn't even know about the lamp yet."

A few minutes later, Jackson, with Mac at his side, stepped off the glass elevator on the thirty-ninth floor. At the end of the hall was a pair of shiny gold doors, and next to it sat a muscled-up bodyguard in a shiny black suit.

They were eight feet from the door when Mr. Muscle stood. Jackson said, "Tell Joe—"

"Don't have to tell Mr. Masado nothing," the man's steroid-inflected voice rumbled. "You and the fur ball have been on camera since you entered the elevator." That said, the guard swung open the heavy bulletproof door to allow them entry.

Jackson stepped inside, and once the *fur ball's* tail

cleared the door, it closed behind them. He glanced around, appreciating Joe's spacious office. The room was first rate, with rich wood walls and a plush carpet. A solid wall of windows overlooked Lake Michigan. Along another wall stood an eighteen-foot bar with an Italian marble surface and six white leather bar chairs fronting it—the gold-framed mirror behind it every bit as long, allowing no one in the room any privacy.

Joe was seated behind a long half-circle desk—five white leather chairs curved around it. He was wearing an expensive gray suit and a smile. Behind him Lucky stood stone sober with a drink in his hand.

What the two Masado brothers shared was equal height—six foot two, to be exact—Sicilian smooth black hair, dark eyes and a straight nose that took center stage on both of their prominent faces. Lucky was thirty-one and Joe was thirty-four, the same age as Jackson.

"What do you think of my elevator, Jacky?" Joe finally asked.

Jackson grinned. "It's bigger than the dream, Joe."

"Yeah. You know how kids are. Ten-story buildings seem plenty big to an eight-year-old."

They shared a laugh while Lucky grunted and tipped up his glass of Scotch. Jackson eyed him, deciding that Lucky needed a new line of work—his job as Frank's soldier was killing him. He was thinner than usual, the chip on his shoulder bigger, and his eyes...his bloodshot eyes were the result of too much booze and not enough sleep.

Jackson asked, "How's life, Lucky?"

"It's a party, Jacky. One big party." He drained

the Scotch. ''Joey filled me in. So how long you staying?''

''For as long as it takes to get Sunni out of the hot seat.''

Unlike Joe's suit-and-tie attire, Lucky wore jeans and a black T-shirt beneath a famous black leather jacket that had a history all its own.

''Have a seat.'' Joey motioned to the leather chairs in front of his eight foot polished oak desk. Jackson left Mac near the door and took a seat while Lucky headed for the bar.

''So what's with the dog, Jacky?''

''He's my partner,'' Jackson answered. ''Can't find anyone who wants to work with me these days but an ornery dog.''

''You saying he'll rip my throat out if you snap your fingers?''

''I don't know. Should we try it and see?''

As Lucky moved to the window behind Joey, carrying another glassful of Scotch, Jackson studied his slow gait, a gait that guaranteed he was in physical pain. Lucky was once as handsome as his older brother, but his street activities had earned him a number of visible scars. But the worst ones were hidden.

Joe, on the other hand, had only one visible scar, but ironically it hadn't come from an enemy's fist or knife. The day he'd told his father he wanted to be an architect instead of a player in the family business, Frank had split his cheek open.

''Sunni came to see me this morning,'' Joey began.

''And?''

''She explained why she'd offered the false information. I've discussed it with Frank. We feel her motivation was solely to benefit Silks, therefore we're willing to work around the problem."

"Which is?"

Joey smiled. "I hear her daddy can be noisy when he's unhappy. We don't want him making noise in Chicago, Jacky. You keep him in New Orleans and we'll be happy."

Jackson nodded. "Okay. Clide stays put. Done."

"Last night you told Joey you'd just gotten into town. This morning I checked that out and learned you've been here five days." Lucky turned from the window. "Why the lie? What's your game, Jacky? And who you playing with?"

Jackson rested his elbow on the arm of the chair. "My game is simple. Find Milo's killer, spring Sunni and head back to New Orleans."

"Why didn't you just come to me?" Joey asked.

"The truth?"

"Always, Jacky."

"I wanted to know who was involved for myself."

"We didn't kill Milo, Jacky."

"I know, but neither did Sunni Blais." Jackson watched Lucky head back to the bar. "About the alibi story..."

"We believe she's innocent, too," Joey said. "It made sense to help her and help ourselves in the process. Masado Towers doesn't need negative publicity."

"No, I suppose not. Can Williams prove the alibi story is a lie?"

"No."

"So now you know whose side we're on," Lucky said from behind the bar.

"The side you've always been on, bro. Frank's."

The blunt statement wasn't meant to start a fire. It was just open and honest. Joe and Lucky had never wanted to be Frank Masado's boys. They had wanted their own identities, their own lives. But being born to *the family* didn't leave them a choice and they all knew it.

As Lucky sat down a few chairs away from Jackson, Joey said, "You've had enough from the bar, *mio fratello.*"

Lucky looked up. "I'm hurting today. Takes the edge off. And even if it didn't, you're my brother, not my mama."

Jackson grinned. Listening to the bickering felt like old times.

Finally, he decided to cut to the chase. "So who killed Milo?"

Joey's eyes traveled to Lucky then back to Jackson. "We don't know. The word on the street is that it wasn't—"

"Anyone we know," Lucky finished.

"Are you sure about that, Lucky?" Jackson persisted.

Lucky licked his lips in anticipation of tasting the alcohol he obviously craved. "If you think I'm guilty of sending that worthless piece of meat to hell, try to prove it, Jacky. Be my guest. Spin your wheels."

"Lucky..." Joey nailed his brother with narrowed eyes. "Unless you want him all over you, back off."

"Him on me?" Lucky snorted. "He can try, but the only way he'd get the jump on me is when I'm hurtin', and then only if he played dirty."

Jackson pulled the knife sheathed at his hip so fast Lucky didn't make a move until it was too late and the wicked blade rested on his jugular.

"God, Jacky! What the hell are you doing?" Joey was on his feet in an instant.

"I'm playing dirty, Joe. What's it look like I'm doing?"

"Dammit, Jacky, that's my brother you're tickling with that thing!"

Before Joey could step around the desk, a low growl filled the room and all eyes moved to Mac as he stalked toward the desk, his lips peeled away from his long, impressive canines.

"Jeez! Call off the dog, Jacky."

Surprised, though not willing to admit it, Jackson watched as Mac turned into one mean son of a bitch—he was a healthy Nine-lives Lucky on four legs. It was the first time the dog had shown any aggression since they'd been teamed up together. Mostly Mac slept, ate and, when he felt an energy surge, chewed up something. "I guess I don't need to snap my fingers," he joked.

"Not funny, Jacky." Joey swore. "This isn't smart, bro."

"If I live through this you're dead," Lucky growled, barely moving a muscle.

"Dammit, Lucky, shut the hell up." Joey's eyes flashed a warning at his brother, then at his friend. "I gave you that Hibben, you son of a bitch. Don't use it on my brother. I'm only going to say it this one time."

It was true the knife had been a gift. A gift Joey had surprised him with on Jackson's eighteenth birthday. "Mac, back off," he ordered. And then, as his partner backtracked three feet, his growl dying slowly, he released Lucky and hurled the expensive Hibben across the room toward the west wall. The deadly knife nailed the mirror behind the bar dead center and shattered glass fell with a loud crash.

Lucky scrambled out of his chair just as the door burst open and Mr. Muscle rushed in waving a sawed-off shotgun. But he didn't get a chance to use the *lupara* before Mac was airborne. Ninety-eight pounds of angry dog hit the stout guard square in the chest and knocked him off balance. A half second later, Mac was all over him, shredding his suit jacket.

Jackson went for the *lupara* on the floor. As he reached for the gun, Lucky said, "Go for it, Jacky. Give me the excuse I don't need."

Jackson spun around to see Lucky aiming a .25 caliber Beretta at his head.

"Dammit!" Joey shouted. "Lucky, pocket that damn thing, then get the hell out of here before you make a mistake you can't live with."

"You want me out?" His look of disbelief matched his mood.

"You need to cool off," Joey insisted.

"Me? What about him? The son of a bitch went for my throat, Joey."

"You were going for mine the minute I walked in the door," Jackson countered.

"Both of you shut up," Joey demanded. "Jacky, sit the hell down. Lucky, go stick your head in a bucket of ice and cool down. Take Gates with you and put him in a new suit."

That wasn't going to happen with Mac standing on his chest. Jackson snapped his fingers and said, "Mac, take a break."

The dog backed off, but instead of taking himself out of the picture entirely, he remained by the door, his eyes glued on Lucky's every move.

Lucky lowered the Italian-made automatic, then suddenly grinned at Jackson. "You've gotten faster, *mio fratello.*" He nodded appreciatively. "That's good. Now I won't worry about you so much."

"You've gotten slower," Jackson countered. "Get rid of the booze, bro."

When they were finally alone, Joey said, "You still drinking beer or do you need something stronger?"

"Beer's good."

"I need a double." Joey crossed to the bar and stepped onto the broken glass to retrieve the drinks and the Hibben.

"You don't drink in the middle of the day," Jackson said as he made himself comfortable in the chair once more.

"Normally I don't need to. Don't do that again, Jacky. Lucky can be a pain in the ass, but he's my pain in the ass. And he's the best reason I've got to get up in the morning. Don't mess with him again."

"He needs to get off the booze."

"That's not news." When Joey returned, he took the chair next to Jackson and handed him first the Hibben, then the beer. "Let's clear the air. You tell me what you've got, and I'll see what I can add to make this mess go away faster."

"What's the story with Lucky?" Jackson asked.

"He's touchy about the murder, but not for the reason you might think. When he learned that Milo had approached Sunni with a partnership deal, he was upset. He confronted Milo and they threw some punches. He was also nervous because we didn't know at that point how Sunni would respond to Milo's offer. But Lucky didn't take out Milo and frame Sunni.'' Joey shook his head. ''That didn't happen, Jacky.''

Jackson tipped back his head and poured the beer down his throat, then took a minute to speculate. Finally he asked, ''When and where did Lucky and Milo face off?''

''Milo's turf.''

''The Shedd?''

Joey nodded. ''Lucky knew better than to go after him there. There are rules, you know. Three days later, Milo's boys hit him when he was leaving the house.''

''The house?''

''He won't stay under Frank's roof, or mine. He moved back to the house in our old neighborhood. He laid unconscious in the alley for two hours, Jacky. When he came to, he dragged himself back inside and called me. When I got there I thought he was dead. I called an ambulance. Ten days later, he walked out of the hospital with only one kidney. A week later Milo turned up dead. I know what it looks like, but Lucky didn't kill him.''

''You know Lucky, Joe. You know he's a hothead.''

''But he's also smart.''

''He used to be smarter than a two-headed cobra. But he's half that man today, Joe.''

''He'll pull it together. He always does.''

''Let's hope it's sooner rather than later.''

''So maybe it's good you're home. You can help me put him back together.''

''What does Frank think?''

Joey snorted. ''Frank's still Frank. For walking out of the hospital in ten days instead of five weeks like the doctor advised, Frank gave Lucky the Beretta he aimed at your head, and two cases of imported Scotch.''

They talked for an hour, reflected on old times—speculated about the future and made some decisions concerning Lucky. When Jackson stood to leave, Joey said, ''It's good to have you home, *mio fratello*. Come, let me show you around.''

The clock on Sunni's desk read three o'clock, marking another wasted hour staring at the stack of paperwork on her desk. She squeezed her eyes shut, chastised herself for wasting precious time, then went right back to daydreaming.

My God, she thought, no man should be allowed to look that good naked. But there it was, the reason she hadn't done an ounce of work all day.

The truth was, her phantom lover was no longer a one-dimensional image. He'd grown legs. He walked. Talked. Had warm lips, and no doubt had the stamina of a bull elk, judging by the visible evidence that had been presented to her that morning. Groaning in frustration, Sunni forced herself to focus on the stack of bills in front of her. Five minutes later—two bills addressed and stamped—a shrill scream from the showroom brought her out of her chair like a rocket.

Moments later she tossed open the door and rushed from her office to see if her manager was all right. But nothing looked amiss—Mary was behind the sales counter waiting on a customer, and the room was dotted with hopefuls. But suddenly another scream sent Sunni's gaze to the left just as something dark dashed under the chemise rack. On recognition, she groaned, then muttered, ''Oh, no…not him again.''

As she muttered the words, Jackson Ward's partner scooted beneath a rack of slips, sent it spinning, then took off to find whatever it was he was looking for. Frozen a few feet from her office door, Sunni watched as he raced past the sales counter, nearly knocking Vetta Samanto onto her rich behind. She squealed, swung her purse, then dug in her heels and clutched the counter.

It suddenly occurred to Sunni that if Mac was there, then Jackson should be somewhere close by. As she scanned the store, she spied him outside in the lobby talking to Joey Masado. They looked like they were in deep conversation, so deep, in fact, that neither one was aware that Mac had wandered off.

She watched Joey suddenly turn and walk off. A second later Jackson turned his gaze around and locked eyes with her. For no sane reason that she could explain, Sunni took a moment to appreciate his broad shoulders in his butter-soft tan shirt, his flat abdomen and sturdy long legs.

Fortunately, or maybe unfortunately, another scream from Vetta sent Sunni's thoughts and her eyes back to the counter, where the determined woman was taking another energetic swing at Mac's head as he raced past her. She missed him by a mile, only this time the swing was healthy enough to knock her off balance and drop her to her knees. As she went down she cried, ''Save us, St. Christopher!''

Jackson arrived at Sunni's side seconds later. ''Hell, I'm sorry. He was supposed to stay with me.''

''You are sooo…dead. Both of you,'' Sunni snapped.

She had no sooner issued the threat when several more screams had them both focusing on the far wall where the dressing rooms were located. All at once the doors shot open as if someone had just signaled the start of the Kentucky Derby, and a dozen Thoroughbred racers left the starting gate in various stages of undress.

"I'm ruined," Sunni groaned as she watched Mac belly-crawl from one dressing room to another like a sniper on a recon mission.

An earsplitting whistle from Jackson brought Mac's head up, his gaze locking on Sunni. As if he'd suddenly found what he was searching for—he bolted toward her like a runaway locomotive that had left the tracks.

"What's he doing?" Sunni asked, taking a step back.

"Hell, I don't know."

"What do you mean, you don't know?" She took another step back. "If he doesn't slow down, he's going to run me over."

Mac achieved warp-speed as he cornered the sales counter. Sunni heard Jackson swear, then she was swept off her feet into his arms and he was scrambling backward several feet.

Mac, who continued to race toward them, suddenly stiffened out his front legs, hauled on the brakes and began to backpedal to keep from colliding into them. At the last minute, he dropped his butt for drag and skidded to a stop mere inches from Jackson's feet.

Seconds later you could have heard a pin drop. Customers stood like statues, their wide eyes glued on Mac sitting in front of them wagging his tail.

It was Saturday, one of the busiest days of the

week. There had to be twenty-plus customers in her little shop. Twenty-plus lost sales who would be issuing complaints to management within the hour.

Finally Mary broke the awkward moment by coming around the counter to help Vetta to her feet. The older woman turned to glare at Sunni, and she opened her mouth to apologize, but Jackson's heavy voice filled the room before she had a chance. "It's all right, folks, the excitement's over now. There was a rabid cat in the building. Our top K-9 was sent in to flush him." He set Sunni on her feet, then flashed his badge too quickly for anyone to dispute his story. "The cat's out of the store, so you can relax. The CPD thanks you for your cooperation, and apologies for any inconvenience we've caused."

His gaze touched on each customer, then he stepped forward, retrieved Vetta's bag off the floor and handed it to her. As he turned, he said loud enough so everyone could hear, "In your office, Miss Blais? A moment of your time."

He took hold of her elbow and steered her into her office. When the door closed behind them, Sunni saw that Mac had followed them and was now wagging his tail. "You," she scolded, "don't you dare look happy. You're a bad dog. Bad dog!"

Mac lowered his head, his tail going still. Sunni instantly felt like an old shrew. "It's not all your fault," she modified, lifting her head to pin Jackson with an accusing glare. "I thought K-9s were well trained. I thought you said he was a veteran. Are you aware that he came—" Sunni held up her hand and measured an inch "—this close to breaking my lamp this morning? And minutes ago, my neck?"

"Since you brought that up. This morning, I mean. I—"

"No. I don't want to talk about this morning." Sunni closed her eyes and tried to calm down. Suddenly she felt a warm thumb brush lightly over her lower lip. She blinked her eyes open and took a step back. "Don't."

"Did anyone ask about that?"

"Mary. I told her I accidently bit myself."

"Bad lie."

"I wouldn't have had to lie at all if you hadn't—" Suddenly a loud rap at the door broke her off. "Yes?"

The door swung open and her manager poked her head in. "There's a Detective Williams here to see you."

Sunni sighed heavily. "All right, Mary. Send him back." When the door closed she said, "That man grilled me for two hours, two different times already. What can I possibly tell him that I haven't told him? Maybe Joey changed his mind and decided to recant his alibi after all. He told me this morning he wouldn't, but—"

"Joe's sticking with the alibi. You don't have to worry about that."

The knock at the door made Sunni jump.

"Let me handle this," he told her.

Sunni nodded, rounded her desk, straightened her suit jacket, then said, "Come in, Detective Williams."

The door opened, and the detective stepped inside. He glanced at Sunni, then at Jackson. Grinning, he said, "The chief told me this morning that you were here. I can't deny I was surprised. Guess I had no idea where you ended up when you left town. Anyway, there's really no need for you to be here. I already told Chief Blais when I learned something I'd shared the info.''

''His daughter's up on a murder charge, Stud. Somehow that doesn't seem like enough. Especially since you think she's guilty.''

''I'm just working with the facts, Jackson.'' Detective Williams glanced at Mac. ''He a better partner than me or Tom? Guess maybe he can dodge bullets a little faster. That's a plus, right?''

Sunni saw Jackson's jaw jerk, but only slightly. He hooked his hip on her desk and fold his arms across his chest. He looked relaxed, and yet far from harmless. ''So what brings you by, Stud? You finally collar the real killer?''

''Not yet.'' He glanced at Sunni. ''I got evidence that proves Milo had a female companion with him before the game ended that night with a bang. I've got Miss Blais's scarves with her prints on them, Jackson. She lives two stories above the crime scene. I got a desk clerk who says she was seen in the elevator three days prior with the deceased and they were arguing.''

''You got a gun?''

''No.''

''Then what you've got, Stud, is circumstantial evidence.'' Jackson reached into his shirt pocket and pulled a piece of paper out. ''Here. This will get you started in the right direction.''

''What's that?''

''I did some legwork for you. There's three suspects, all with solid motives.''

For a long minute Detective Williams didn't move,

then finally he accepted the paper. As he studied the list, Sunni studied him from over Jackson's left shoulder. The Chicago detective was good-looking, had broad shoulders, wore his blond hair in a crew cut and had Nordic blue eyes. He was clean and dressed in a suit jacket and tie over a white shirt and dark slacks. Sunni estimated him to be close to Jackson Ward's age.

After he'd scanned the list, he looked up and said, "I would have thought at least one Masado would have made your list. Why not?"

"Too obvious."

"And why should I check out Vincent D'Lano?"

"Milo stole the waterfront property out from under him. The lot where the Shedd sits and the one next to it."

"And how did you find that out?"

Jackson shrugged.

"Why should I believe you got the facts straight, and that you're not covering for her and trying to score points with your boss?"

"Because you're a fool if you think that, Stud, and you were never a fool. Just a little slow at the bar when it came to tipping jiggers."

Stud grinned, his gaze finally finding Sunni. "Sorry, Miss Blais. Didn't mean to ignore you. I've come to ask you a few more questions." Jackson shook his head. "She's not answering anything, Stud. Not without her lawyer."

"If she's innocent, she won't mind answering a few. Isn't that right, Miss Blais?"

"Ask your questions, Detective."

Jackson turned and gave Sunni the evil eye. She gave it back.

Detective Williams pulled a notepad from his pocket. "Is it true Elizabeth Carpenter was an employee of yours?"

"Yes."

"And she worked for you for how long?"

"Two weeks."

"Was there a problem? Two weeks is a short time."

"The job was a few days a week. She wanted a full-time position."

"And she found it?"

"Yes, but she never said where." Sunni suddenly became worried. "What's this all about, Detective? Is something wrong with Elizabeth?"

"Her employer filed a missing-person report this morning."

Sunni sucked in her breath. "I don't understand."

Jackson asked, "Who's her employer, Stud?"

"The Shedd. She's been an exotic dancer there since last September. She was Milo's favorite. Her stage name was Libby."

It was after seven when Jackson returned to his apartment at the Wilchard. After leaving Silks that afternoon, he'd set out to find Elizabeth Carpenter. He'd turned over every rock and talked to everyone who knew her, but the twenty-two-year-old dancer who supported her drug habit on the runway at the Shedd was definitely missing.

Jackson entered the bedroom and went straight to the window. Gazing across the alley, he expected to see lights on in Sunni's apartment, but when he didn't, his eyebrows lifted. Before he'd left her office, he'd ordered her to go straight home. She'd agreed she would.

He lit up a cigarette and took a hard drag, then sent the smoke out the open window. Mac appeared at his side, and as he reached out and stroked the dog's head he recalled Mac's impressive performance in Joe's office, and then his crazy antics at Silks a few hours later.

The file on Mac had claimed he was a Super Dog at one time. Jackson had found that hard to believe after living with the lazy mutt—if Mac wasn't sleeping, he was chewing up a T-shirt or the leg off a chair. But today he'd witnessed ninety-eight pounds of K-9 aggression come alive like a demon from hell. It was almost as if Mac had been running on empty, and then somewhere between the first and the thirty-ninth floor of Masado Towers someone had fed him a four-pack of Energizers.

He admitted he had a new respect for the dog after seeing him in action. He wondered if he was on a comeback, and if that was true, what had caused it.

He checked his watch, then eyed Sunni's dark apartment. Suddenly anxious, he gave Mac a nudge with his knee. "Go check it out. See if she forgot to lock the slider again. See what you can find out."

As if Mac was just waiting for the go-ahead, he jumped through the open window and trotted down the fire escape, then leapt to the alley. Seconds later, he scaled the iron stairs up the side of the Crown Plaza and vaulted onto Sunni's terrace.

It had started to rain, a cold fall rain that put a definite chill in the air. Jackson watched through the rain as Mac nudged at the slider, and sure enough, it opened.

As Mac disappeared inside, Jackson's cell phone rang. He considered ignoring it. What if it was Clide? He wasn't up to talking to his boss, especially when, at the moment, he couldn't tell him precisely where his daughter was. On the other hand, maybe it was one of his old contacts. Maybe they had found out something more on Elizabeth Carpenter's disappearance.

On the fifth ring, Jackson pulled his phone from his pocket. "Ward here."

"Jackson?"

"Sis?"

"Can you come get me? They won't let me leave unless—"

"Where are you?"

"I'm at Northwestern Memorial."

"The hospital? Why? What happened?"

"Just come. I'll explain when you get here. Hurry, can you?"

When the phone went dead, Jackson jammed it into his pocket, then went to the window and gave a shrill whistle. A few seconds later, Mac was back on Sunni's terrace. He motioned to the dog, and in minutes Mac was on the move, racing down the fire escape and heading back to the Wilchard.

Chapter 7

The bad news was that the cab driver was in surgery. The good news was Sunni had escaped the accident without any serious injuries.

She checked her watch and wondered how long it would take Jackson to get there. She'd had mixed emotions about calling him. But someone had just played Russian roulette with her life on the freeway and she would be a fool to dismiss the incident as just a freak accident.

She wrapped her arms around herself and watched the minutes on the clock slowly tick by. When the emergency door opened a little while later, she shot her head up, only to be disappointed when the man who stepped into the room was Detective Williams.

"You were luckier than the cab driver, Miss Blais."

"Yes, I was," she agreed. "He's still in surgery."

"You told the officer at the scene of the accident

that you believe the car deliberately sideswiped the cab. Is that true?''

''Yes.''

He dug in his pocket for his notepad. ''Can you fill me in on what happened?''

Sunni let out a tired sigh and regretted it. Even the slightest movement sent pain shooting throughout her entire body. She moaned inwardly and gripped the edge of the examining table she was sitting on. ''Can't you talk to the officer I spoke with earlier? He wrote down what I said.''

''Oh, you can bet I'll talk to him. But I want to hear it from you firsthand. If this was no accident then maybe I've been wrong about you, Miss Blais.''

Glad to hear that, Sunni told the detective that she'd left Masado Towers at five-thirty like usual. She'd hailed a cab and was headed home when a black car suddenly appeared and swerved into them, forcing the cab into a concrete divider.

''Can you give a description of the driver?''

''No. The car windows were tinted black.''

''You said the car swerved into the cab. Could the car have been changing lanes, and—''

''No. If it had been an accident, he wouldn't have fled the scene, would he?''

''People panic. It's a common reaction. You used the word 'he.' I thought you said you couldn't see who was driving.''

''I couldn't.''

''Then using *he* is speculation, Ms. Blais. It suggests you saw the driver.'' He looked up from scribbling something down on his pad. ''But you say you didn't see the driver.''

''No.''

"I suppose you didn't get the license plate number?"

"No."

"This isn't much to go on. Let's hope the cab driver pulls through and has something to add."

Sunni felt dizzy. She closed her eyes, trying to think rationally. She heard the door, and she blinked her eyes open, relieved to see Jackson with Mac beside him.

She was sitting on the examination table with her feet dangling two feet off the floor. Her gray silk skirt was blood-stained from trying to help the cab driver before the ambulance had arrived. She'd lost her white silk scarf and the end result was too much cleavage. Only that didn't matter, all that mattered was that Jackson had come to take her home.

His eyes met hers, and then he was crossing the room, planting himself directly in front of her. It was so strange to feel such utter relief, but that's exactly what she felt as his big hands brushed her hair away from her face. "You hurt?"

"No. Just a few bruises."

The heat from his hand on her face as he examined the bruise on her forehead was shockingly soothing. His hip leaned into her thigh, and that, too, was comforting.

"What do you got, Stud?" he asked, not turning around.

"Hit and run, or attempted murder. Can't say just yet."

Mac decided he'd been ignored too long, and he leapt up on the table and sat next to her. "Hi, Mac," Sunni whispered, then leaned into the dog's shoulder.

He leaned back—his sturdy body supporting her—and bent his head to nuzzle her ear.

His fur was wet. She asked, "Is it raining?"

"Started about an hour ago." Finally Jackson turned to Detective Williams. "Got a lead on the car yet? A license plate number?"

"Miss Blais didn't get the plate number. We're going to have to wait until the cab driver comes around. Right now we don't have much. Maybe you were right. Maybe there's more to this than we first thought."

"We?" Jackson shook his head. "You mean, *you* first thought."

"Okay. Have it your way. You always did when we were working together. Why should anything change now?"

"So we're sharing information. Is that it?"

"Makes sense."

"Take down my cell number so you can reach me day or night."

Jackson recited the phone number while Detective Williams wrote it down. Then Stud said, "Here's mine. If Miss Blais remembers something, I'd appreciate hearing about it. Need a lift home?"

"No. We'll catch a cab," Jackson said.

When Detective Williams walked out and closed the door, Sunni sighed. "Can I go home now?"

"Not a problem, Sis. Put your arms around my neck, and we're out of here." As she raised her arms, he scooped her up and drew her against his broad chest. Then they were on the move, heading out of the emergency room with Mac trotting to keep up with Jackson's long stride.

* * *

Jackson unlocked the apartment after setting Sunni on her feet. He pocketed the key, shoved the door open, then once more lifted her. "Arms around my neck," he instructed again.

"Wait. No, you don't have to… Really I'm fine."

"You're not fine. Besides, why walk when you can ride?"

He swept her through the door and kicked it shut behind him. He was about to flick on the light when he remembered the busted lamp that used to sit behind one of the sofas. Tomorrow would be soon enough to explain about the lamp, he decided, then started down the dark hall to her bedroom.

She had scared the hell out of him when she'd called from the hospital. He'd worried all the way over in the cab. And he'd nearly taken off the receptionist's head at the front desk when she'd directed him to the emergency department.

"I can walk now," she whispered against his cheek. Her fingers were laced around his neck, her touch doing crazy things to his insides. "You don't need to spend the energy. I'll be your legs tonight."

Relying on the small security light on the terrace, Jackson walked into her bedroom without mishap and made his way to her bed in the center of the room. He laid her down, and on hearing her moan, said, "Sorry, Sis."

"Don't be. This wasn't your fault."

"Wasn't it?" Jackson jaw jerked as he sat down beside her.

"Don't do the guilt thing, okay? You're suppose to be a snake with no morals, remember?"

"I shouldn't have left you alone."

''You can't be with me every minute.''

That was where she was wrong. But Jackson kept his thoughts to himself as he reached for the light next to the bed and turned it on. As he glanced around the room, the first thing he noticed was the massive iron canopy overhead and the sheer curtains at each corner, then how beautiful and sexy Sunni Blais looked lying on the pale green comforter.

The walls had been washed with a textured colorless paint. The main color in the room was a pale green. White roses in a tall vase were reflected in the mirror on the vanity. The carpet was as pale as the walls and the painted iron bed. A paneled mirror along an entire wall doubled as doors to what must be her closet. Like the one that encompassed the ceiling inside her shower in the bathroom, this mirror captured the bed like a wide-angle camera lens.

Jackson had never been so aware or so affected by a woman, or her sexuality, before he'd met Sunni Blais. The truth was his senses had sharpened in all directions where she was concerned. And everything about her turned him on—her body, the smell of her skin, her husky voice, her slippery clothes, her home full of mirrors.

He stood and removed her silver shoes. ''You missed dinner, right?''

''No. I had a sandwich brought into my office around five. I don't usually do that but... Well, I just felt hungry. But not now.''

''I'm going to have to call your father.''

''I wish you wouldn't. He's supposed to leave the hospital in a few days. This could set him back.''

''Keeping secrets isn't a good idea, Sis.''

"Sometimes it's better than the truth. In this case, I know I'm right." She winced as she tried to sit up.

"Don't move. You don't have a reason to get up. I'm your legs tonight, remember? What do you need?"

"I need to call Mary." She sank back against the pillows and closed her eyes. "I want to tell her I won't be in to work tomorrow until afternoon."

"I'll call." Jackson rounded the bed. "But I'll tell her you're not coming in for at least two days. Maybe three."

Her pretty gray eyes popped open. "I have to work."

"Mary's more than capable of running the store. I'll keep an eye on her for you. Here, let me help you out of your clothes."

He reached out to slip open the top button on her jacket, but she stopped him by grabbing his hand. "I can manage."

"Come on, Sis. I've seen you before, remember?"

She pushed his hand away, her own floating upward to cover her cleavage. "We're strangers, Jackson, I—"

"A stranger couldn't automatically find a frying pan in your kitchen, or a towel in the bathroom without a search. I can. A stranger wouldn't be aware of your little problem, either."

"My problem…"

Jackson pointed to her hand, which she was using to shield her breasts from his eyes. "The *twins*. You don't like drawing attention to them."

"The *twins?* You've named my—"

"They're twins, right? One isn't weird or a pound

or two larger or smaller.'' Jackson shrugged out of his jacket and tossed it to the floor.

''A pound or two larger or smaller?''

''Yeah. I knew this girl once who... Well, never mind. Where's that robe you were wearing this morning? Do you hang something like that or drawer it?''

''Hang. But—''

He found the small knob that buckled the mirrored closet doors and folded them accordion style out of the way. When he spied the blue robe he remembered from that morning, he reached for it. The minute his fingers wrapped around it, he was reminded of how super-soft and sexy all of Sunni's clothes were.

''Can't you find it?''

''I found it. You like silk, I take it?'' He closed the closet doors, and when he turned, Sunni was sitting up.

''Silk is my business. It reminds me of the petals on a rose.'' She paused, gazed at his hand holding her robe. ''Just lay it on the bed. I'll take it from here.''

''First, prove to me you can stand up.''

''Of course I can stand.''

Jackson offered her a doubtful raised eyebrow, then tossed the robe over his shoulder. Hands on his hips, he said, ''Show me.''

''I'm not helpless.''

''Show me.''

She inched herself off the bed, her toes reaching for the floor. As they made contact with the carpet, Jackson knew her legs weren't going to hold her up. He saw her left knee buckle just as he reached out to her and she reached out to him. He heard her swear softly as he caught her around the waist and dragged her up his body and held her close.

"Don't you dare say anything," she muttered against his chest.

"I wasn't going to."

She kept her face tight against his chest, her hands gripping his forearms. "This is embarrassing."

"Don't waste your energy being embarrassed, Sis. It's just you and me here. And I never kiss and tell."

His comment brought her head up. "I don't even know you, and here you are, in my bedroom. Going through my closet. And—"

"Don't forget this morning I was in your kitchen and your shower."

His teasing made her cheeks turn pink. "I'm sorry about…you know, bursting into the bathroom. I really thought Mac was going to break my expensive lamp."

Jackson winced inwardly, keying on the word *expensive.* He had figured it was something special. He pushed the lamp from his mind and concentrated on putting Sunni's mind to rest about the bathroom ordeal. He reached up and brushed his thumb over her still-swollen lower lip. "Like now, Sis, this morning was just you and me. No one's going to hear any of it from me."

"But I barely know you, and—"

"You know me," he said softly. "I'm the guy you called tonight when you needed someone you could count on. I'm the guy who raced to the hospital. The guy who tipped the cab driver fifty bucks to get me there in ten minutes."

She let go of his arms, forced her legs to hold her up. "Fifty dollars?"

Jackson nodded. ‘‘Looks like I’m going to have to tighten up my leash on you from now on, or go broke tipping cabbies.’’

‘‘And what does that mean, exactly?’’

He brushed his knuckles across her cheek. He shouldn’t be touching her so much, but he couldn’t stop. ‘‘I want you close from now on,’’ he told her. ‘‘What happened tonight can’t happen again.’’ *Or he was going to start growing ulcers like Clide.*

‘‘Close? What does that mean?’’

‘‘Tonight was no accident. We both know that. I want you to agree to whatever I think is necessary from here on out.’’

‘‘Without knowing what it is first?’’ She shook her head. ‘‘I don’t think I can do that.’’

‘‘I need to know your every move until I learn more about this case.’’

‘‘You think I’m next, don’t you?’’

The worry in her eyes slipped into her voice. Jackson wrapped his arms around her, trying to be as brotherly as possible. He felt her shudder, and he drew her closer. As he offered her more of his body, she curled her arms around his waist and exhaled shakily. They stood that way for several minutes before he gently set her away from him. ‘‘I don’t know you’re a target, Sis. But I don’t know that you’re not, either. Now, you change and get into bed. I’ll go call Mary, then check on Mac and make sure that he’s behaving himself. If you need me, yell. I’ll leave the door open.’’

It was the headache that woke her, but it was her tingling lips that forced Sunni into action. Ignoring her sore, protesting muscles, she sat up and turned on her bedside lamp. Seconds later, she had her second drawer open and she was assessing her snacks.

It was no surprise that she was fighting bouts of hypoglycemia. Routine-wise, her body had been on a roller coaster ride for days.

She withdrew her glucose sensor and record book from the drawer, then tested her blood. In a matter of minutes she had her answer and a small box of raisins in her hand. Resting her head and back against a pillow, she patiently munched on the sweet fruit.

A short time later, feeling better, she glanced at the luminous face on the crystal clock next to the light. It read 2:00 a.m. She'd slept close to four hours—fitfully, but she had slept.

The apartment was quiet, which was normal, but she couldn't help wondering if Jackson and Mac were still there. Determined to find out, she eased herself out of bed—stifling a moan as she straightened in small doses. Pressing her hand to her lower back, and in a movement that resembled Edna's famous slipper-shuffle, she retrieved her blue robe draped across the bed, then gritted her teeth as she forced her arms up to slip it on over her white chemise and matching panties.

She left the bedroom taking baby steps, tying the belt around her waist. Light drew her eye to the kitchen, and to Sunni's surprise and relief, Jackson was seated at the table with a laptop computer in front of him. A pile of papers was stacked on one side of the computer and a *man-size* coffee mug—resembling nothing in her kitchen cupboards—was on the other side.

"Do you know what time it is?"

He looked up from the computer. "Time for you to be fast asleep, Sis. Why aren't you?"

"It's my back. It's killing me. I can't get comfortable."

He shoved the chair back and stood. That's when Sunni noticed his shirt was unbuttoned. Thc tails were out of his jeans, and it allowed her a grand view of his sun-bronzed hairy chest and flat, slab-of-steel belly. He wore a silver chain around his neck with a stylized cross of some kind hanging from it. His feet were bare, and his jeans were unbuttoned.

Even feeling as lousy as she did, she couldn't help but admire his rugged body, or the fact that each and every time she saw him, she had this incredible urge to reach out and touch him.

"Probably a pulled muscle. Got an ice pack?"

"Hmm... Oh, in the freezer."

He sauntered to the fridge and opened the freezing compartment, and was back in a few seconds with the cold pack and a towel he'd fetched from a drawer.

"Do you know where everything in my kitchen is?" she asked.

"All except the popcorn popper and the blender."

"I don't use either of those items."

"No popper?"

"I use microwave popcorn. And I gave my blender to Edna. I never used it."

Sunni dismissed the cold pack when he held it out to her, and shuffled past him to the table. "This is the case information you've collected so far?"

"That's it. I hope you don't mind that I turned your kitchen into an office for tonight. I went back to my apartment and picked up a few things. I didn't leave you alone. Mac stood guard."

"Where is Mac now?"

"Asleep on the terrace. He likes it out there."

Sunni eyed the impressive stack of papers. To have this much information on a case in such a short time took a huge amount of work. "You haven't slept much since you got here, have you?"

"Why do you say that?"

"I'm a cop's kid, remember? It takes hours of legwork to come up with all this."

"I've never needed much sleep. Five hours and I'm good."

Sunni turned to look at him. He was *good* all right. Good-looking, a good cook… And from what she'd seen of him below the waist that morning, she now knew that Jackson Ward had potential in another area as well.

"Sis?"

"Hmm…?"

"Come on. I'll put you back in bed with this ice pack."

Sunni blinked out of her naughty muse. "I can't lie flat. It hurts too bad." She pressed her fingers into her backbone at waist level and grimaced. "Maybe I could sleep in a chair."

"You can't sleep in a chair. Here, let me take a look. Maybe a vertebra was injured in the accident."

"No. The doctor took an X ray. He said it was just bruised." She turned to read the laptop screen. "Vito Tandi's worth sixty million?"

"That's what he admits to." His answer was right next to her ear. A second later one hand settled on her hip, while the other reached around her and laid the cold pack on the table next to the stack of papers. "What do you think is going on…with your back?"

He may as well have asked what do you think is going on with us? Because they both knew something had changed between them since she'd called him on his cell phone and he'd raced to the hospital. "I don't know" was her staid answer. "It just hurts."

"Let's see what I can see."

Sunni's hands instinctively gripped the edges of her robe. "No!"

He covered her hands, pulled them away from her body and laid them palm-side down on the table. "Relax, Sis," he whispered, then gently moved his fingers up her spine, pressing gently on each vertebra as his hand climbed slowly upward. "No pain in your neck?"

"No."

His fingers started back down, again checking out each vertebra. Sunni could hear him breathing, feel his heat. Her own heart was pounding faster than normal.

"Breathe, Sis, you're not breathing. In and out, in and out. Come on."

Feeling foolish, she exhaled and started to breathe. When his fingers moved past her waistline, she let out a scream. "Ouch!"

"There?" His fingers stopped just above her tailbone and gently tested the tender spot.

"That's it. Ooh…careful."

He dropped his hands. "I want to see. Get rid of the robe."

"My robe?"

His arms came around her quickly and untied the slippery silk belt before she could get her hands off the table. A second after that, the robe was peeled off her shoulders and went sailing past her to the chair on the far side of the table. It caught on the back of the chair, then slid out of sight into the seat.

"Jackson, wait. I don't have—"

"Sssh. It's just me, remember?"

His hands reached for the edge of her white chemise. Then without warning, he squatted down, bringing his face mere inches from Sunni's backside—her *exposed* backside. That's right, she wore the latest fashion in underwear. The white silk thong was worth forty dollars and fit her like a glove. Something he would have known if he had given her time to explain.

Sunni squeezed her eyes shut and waited. A full minute passed and still he didn't say anything. Finally she said, "Well...what do you see? I mean... You're down there to look at my sore back, remember?"

"I remember why I'm down here."

His heavy voice sounded huskier, and a bit strained. A second later, she felt his fingers slide over her spine and gently probe the sensitive areas above her tailbone. He said, "Slightly swollen. A damn good bruise." He dropped her chemise back into place, then stood and took the cold pack wrapped in the small towel off the table and gently pressed it to the injured area. "It'll be a few days before you feel like racing me to the elevator."

"Jack...son, I—"

"Nice drawers."

"Why did I know you were going to mention my underwear?"

"Because if I think it, I say it. Nice butt, too. Real nice."

Sunni sucked in her breath, then let it out slowly as the cold pack began to ease her pain.

"Here." He took a step closer, his arm coming around the front of her to rest on her stomach. Pressing gently, he eased her back so her shoulders rested on his chest and the cold pack was wedged tightly between them. "Relax into me," he softly said next to her ear. "Yeah, that's it. Right there."

For the next several minutes neither one spoke. Eyes closed, Sunni tried to remember to keep breathing. Finally, she said, "We can't stand like this all night."

"I know. I've got an idea. Want to hear it?"

She really did like his voice.

"Sis, you sleeping standing up?"

"No. But I wish I could."

"Let's go in the bedroom."

His suggestion sent Sunni's eyes blinking open. "The bedroom?"

"I don't have to see your face to know what you're thinking. Shame on you. You're suppose to be hurtin'. Or are you pulling my leg?"

Sunni was glad he couldn't see her face, her cheeks felt hot. She could barely walk; of course he wasn't suggesting anything sexual. "Do you enjoy making me uncomfortable?"

"You're fun to tease. You wear your feelings. It's pretty entertaining at times."

"And you never wears yours? This cold pack, *'yeah, that's it. Right there,'* is all for me, right?"

He chuckled. "Smart lady."

"What's your idea?"

"I think if I show you it'll be better." He eased her away from him and shut down his computer. He turned off the kitchen light next. "Here." He handed her the cold pack, then carefully, without warning, he lifted her and cradled her against him. Again Sunni wrapped her arms around his neck the way she'd done earlier.

In her room, he eased her down on the edge of the bed. "Sit there a minute," he said, then pulled the comforter back and stacked two pillows against the iron headboard. When he was finished, he climbed onto the bed and lay down. Spreading his long legs wide, he put the third pillow in the notch. "Okay, now it's your turn."

Sunni stared at the open space. "You want me…there?" She pointed to the open vee.

"We'll fit the ice to your back when you get into position, and I'll pull the comforter over us to keep you warm."

Sunni studied the situation a minute longer.

"If we're lucky, I'll fit you like a glove, Sis, and be the perfect medicine for what ails you. In two days, three at the most, you can kick me out of your bed and have it all to yourself again."

He wanted her to sleep between his rock-hard thighs for two or three days? He had to be joking.

He yawned, patted the pillow. "Come on. Try me out and see how I fit."

This was crazy. Utterly insane. Nonetheless, Sunni slowly got onto all fours and crawled into the open notch between Jackson's legs. Then, before she slid into position, he adjusted the cold pack to her lower back.

A minute passed before she let herself relax fully against him, two minutes before she allowed herself to rest her head on his bare chest. He covered her with the blanket seconds later.

"Jackson, can you sleep like this all night?"

His response was slow in coming. It came after he'd shifted slightly and made a few minor adjustments. "I'm the whatever-it-takes cop, remember? I'll manage. Now, get some sleep, Sis."

Chapter 8

Jackson shrugged into his jacket, glad he had an appointment to keep. For two days he'd been cooped up with Sunni in her apartment, sharing her space during the daylight hours, and sleeping with her between his legs each night. And he was headed for an early grave if he had to sleep as her backboard one more night, harder than a steel pipe.

He'd endured naked lovers etched on glass shower doors, mirrors on the ceiling, a canopy bed straight out of a fairy tale. Sunni in silk at breakfast. Sunni in silk on the sofa. Sunni in silk between his legs all night long.

The ordeal had likely caused him permanent damage—a man's anatomy wasn't meant to be primed like Old Faithful, twenty-four hours a day without some kind of pressure release. And there would be no release as long as he stayed in her apartment. What he needed was a breath of cold reality back in his lungs, along with some good old-fashioned Chicago smog.

In the kitchen Jackson poured his man-size mug full of coffee. As he turned to leave, he locked eyes with Sunni on the other side of the counter—today's silk torture was the color of fresh peaches, and as usual, she looked good enough to eat.

"Where are you going?"

"I've got an appointment this morning."

"You never mentioned an appointment last night. With who?"

Jackson pointed to the piece of paper on the counter. "I explained it in the note."

She glanced at the paper, then eyed his coffee mug. "Do all cops drink as much coffee as you do?"

If they were trying to cut back on their smoking they did. He'd decided this was as good a time as any to chuck the habit. Only with the situation being what it was lately, he really didn't need another added frustration.

"I called the hospital and checked on the cab driver this morning. He's out of intensive care. I'm going over there to talk to him."

She stepped around the counter and walked past him, depositing that feminine scent of hers on the end of his nose. She was moving better than she had for the past two days. Good, maybe tonight he'd be able to get some real sleep.

She glanced at the stove. "Didn't you make breakfast?"

"Yeah. I already ate."

"But I haven't."

The look of disappointment she offered him made

him feel guilty. "Maid service is going to start costing you pretty soon, Sis."

"Maid service?" She lifted an irritated brow. "I can cook."

"You haven't for two days." He eyed the twins, felt old faithful on the rise.

"That's because I haven't been able to buy space in my kitchen."

"Well today you're in luck. I'm going to be gone all day." Jackson headed out of the kitchen with his mug of coffee. "About Mac… I want you to forgive him for breaking your lamp, and let him come back inside."

"There's no way."

Mac had lost ground with Sunni when she'd noticed her expensive lamp wasn't behind the sofa two days ago. And when Jackson'd showed her what was left of it—the pieces he'd boxed up that were out on the terrace—she had kicked Mac out to join the box of broken glass. Mac had been sleeping, and eating, and pouting out on the terrace ever since. And Sunni had been doing pretty much the same inside.

Jackson faced her. "I want him inside today."

"No."

"If he's going to be any use to you, he needs to be inside. I can't leave you if you don't agree." When she said nothing, he softened his voice, "Come on, Sis, lighten up. I'll buy you another lamp."

"You won't buy me another Calafar. It was a one-of-a-kind."

Her hands went to her trim waist, parting the silk robe. The twins sprang forward and damn near waved, giving Jackson a generous amount of cleavage to drool over. He'd been doing so damn much drooling lately that he was in danger of dehydrating.

"I've got to go," he said, disgustedly. "I made egg soufflé last night while you were in the shower. It's in the fridge. All you have to do is heat it up in the microwave."

"You made breakfast last night?"

The surprise in her voice and her appreciative smile sent another surge of heat into Jackson's groin. He liked making her happy, and that was a dangerous thing. He swore softly, then headed for the door. "Make up with Mac, and keep him with you. He'll do you more good than that .22 you got in your jewelry box."

"You know what's in my jewelry box?"

She had followed him to the door, her cream-complexion suddenly pale. "Why the surprised look? What are you hiding, Sis? You suddenly look like white paint in a blackout."

"I'm not hiding anything."

"Maybe I should go through your drawers and see for myself."

"I'm not hiding anything," she said more insistently.

"No whips or chains? Maybe a black leather thong?"

His teasing fell flat. "I sell silk, not a trip to the dungeon."

Her pretty mouth settled into a full pout. Jackson had the urge to lower his head and taste her. Instead he glanced at his watch. "Get Mac in here as soon as I leave. Don't go anywhere. And call me on my cell if you need something. Soufflé takes two minutes in the microwave. Fresh orange juice is in the fridge."

"Juice? You made me juice?"

Another smile. He opened the door and stepped into the hall. "I checked with Mary at Silks. She's going to call you. The Paris Plus supers are on back order."

"Oh, no. The bras or the panties?"

Her innocent question sent Jackson's gaze to the *twins.* He had never in his life wanted to touch a woman as much as he wanted to touch Sunni Blais. Touch her, hell—*smother* her was more like it.

"Jackson, did you hear me?"

"Ah...bras." He reached out, then dropped his hand. "Let Mac in," he grumbled. "Promise me."

She was staring at him, her eyes searching. Suddenly she reached up and slid her hands inside his jacket to straighten his shirt collar. Patting his chest with a look of approval for her efforts, she said, "All right. He's in. But I can't guarantee what kind of mood I'll be in when you get back."

He had to get out of there. "Watch TV with him," he offered. "He likes dog shows and the cooking channel."

Jackson slipped into the white two-story house by way of the unlocked back door, and a hundred memories came rushing back. He glanced around Tom Mallory's kitchen and almost expected to hear his ex-partner's voice. But it wasn't Tom seated at the table waiting for him. The man who had left the door unlocked and a message on Jackson's cell phone was Police Chief Hank Mallory, Tom's father.

They hadn't spoken in three years. The last time had been an explosive shouting match that had ended with Hank throwing an angry punch—a punch that had split Jackson's lip and broken his cheekbone. He'd worn both to Tom's funeral two days later.

As the door banged shut, Hank brought his head around from staring out the window. "When I heard you were in town and why...I guess you'd be Chief Blais's likely choice. He must be pretty upset over this situation with his daughter. Heard he's laid up in the hospital, to add to his upset."

Hank looked like he'd aged ten years instead of three, Jackson thought. He was a big man, and at one time had been athletic. But for years he'd sat behind a desk and the inactivity had made him teddy-bear soft around the middle. His hair was completely gray and the lines around his pale blue eyes told the story of a man who had lost too much in too short a time.

"New Orleans agree with you?"

"It'll do." Jackson stood just inside the door. "The heat's a bitch, but if a man doesn't like things, he changes them, or not. Either way, life goes on."

"Feeling the heat means you're alive. My son doesn't feel anything anymore."

It was still there between them, the old pain and resentment. Maybe it would always be there. He was alive, and Tom was dead. Hank was bitter and he had every right to be.

"I was way out of line that day." Hank's gaze went back out the window. "I regret a lot of things I said. Blaming you for Tom's death most of all."

Jackson stepped further into the room and leaned against the kitchen counter. "He was my friend, as well as my partner. He was shot in the back in a dirty alley. I wish I could have been there. You were right. Maybe if I had been things would have turned out different."

Hank turned to give Jackson his full attention. ''I have information for you that concerns the Tandi case. We could have done this in my office, but I wanted… I wanted to see you in private.'' He motioned to the letter on the table. ''A few days ago that was mailed to the precinct.''

Jackson crossed to the table and picked up the letter. Unfolding it, he read the brief paragraph, his eyebrows lifting slightly. ''So someone thinks the war between Vito Tandi and Frank Masado has been resurrected?''

''Vito's been a recluse for twenty-five years, but everyone knows he's sitting in that big house pushing buttons. He's been trying to take over Frank Masado's empire for years. Maybe Frank just got tired of looking over his shoulder and hit Milo to force Vito out in the open.''

It wasn't a new idea. He'd already examined that theory, but he didn't think that's why Milo was dead. ''Why now?'' Jackson asked. ''A lot of years have gone by. And then there's the organization to consider. A house divided makes them weak. Sure, there's fighting going on inside, but a hit on one of their own? I don't know.''

''Men like Frank Masado and Vito Tandi never forgive or forget. I've never questioned the rumors. I believe Vito sent his wife to the bottom of Lake Michigan because she betrayed him with his best friend. And likewise, I believe Frank Masado loved Grace Tandi or he wouldn't have jeopardized everything to be with her. Living with a powerful amount of hate can make a man do terrible things. Things he regrets, but can never change.''

Jackson studied his ex-boss, wondering if Hank

was speaking from personal experience or case history. He had taken Tom's death hard, as he should have, but he'd wanted revenge afterwards, not justice. And there was a difference.

"You still tight with the Masado boys?"

"Joe and Lucky aren't involved in this, Hank. If they had wanted Milo dead they would have taken him for a ride a long time ago."

"Then how about D'Lano?"

"It's possible, but Vincent D'Lano owns a salvage yard. Why not just drop two tons of steel on Milo? No body, no investigation. He's on my suspect list, but I'm starting to think the person who killed Milo has an altogether different agenda." Jackson pulled out a chair and sat opposite Hank. "This letter...any prints?"

"No. It's been analyzed. Handwriting suggests it was written by a woman." Hank turned to stare out the window once more. "Looks like I need to mow the lawn again."

Jackson glanced out the window. The lawn did need to be mowed, and the toolshed repainted. He leaned back in his chair and surveyed the kitchen. Everything appeared to be just like he remembered—there were even clean dishes in the dish drainer. That had been Tom's pet peeve about Jackson. Jackson liked a clean kitchen—the dishes in the cupboards—and Tom thought putting dishes away was a waste of time when you were just going to use them again a few hours later. "I expected you would have sold this place by now."

"Not yet. Not until I know who killed my boy and why."

"Still want revenge, Hank?"

Hank laughed bitterly. "Yes, I can't deny I want blood."

Jackson never liked dancing around what was on his mind. Straightforward is the way he liked things. Straight, clean and honest. "What's going on, Hank? Why did you want to meet me here?"

Hank closed his eyes a minute. Finally, when he opened them, he said, "There's been talk that Tom was on the take. That he was seeing some woman who was connected to the organization. The rumor claims he was hit because he was a dirty cop messing where he didn't belong."

"That's bull," Jackson responded quickly. "There was no way Tom was dirty."

"That letter isn't much. It was an excuse to see you." Hank smiled sadly. "I suppose you figured that out by now. What I really wanted to talk to you about was Tom. I wanted to hear you say it wasn't true. And to ask a favor."

"Ask it, Hank. Whatever you need."

"If while you're here you find out anything about Tom, I'd like to be the first to know. Good or bad, I need to know first. Will you agree to that?"

"He wasn't dirty, Hank. But if I learn something, I'll tell you first."

"Here, take this." He pulled a key from his shirt pocket and laid it on the table. "In case we need to meet again. Now what about this woman, Clide Blais's daughter?"

"What about her?"

"How's she holding up?"

"She's a cop's kid. She's smart. She'll be all right."

"I got a look at her that morning she was brought

in for questioning. She's not only smart, she's easy on the eyes."

"She's all of that," Jackson agreed.

"That's it? You're not going to say anything more?" Hank grinned. "Why do I take that to mean something?"

Jackson shrugged.

"Are you on a diet?"

"No."

"Then you haven't really looked at her? Those curves?"

Oh, yeah, he'd *really* looked at her, Jackson mused. He'd had plenty of opportunity to look at her from all angles the past two days. And no one needed to tell him how remarkable Sunni's curves were, or how fabulous she smelled. They'd been sandwiched together like sardines. They'd been so damn close that they'd been recycling the same air. The same heat.

"The house is yours while you're here if you want it. Feel free to move in if it works for you." Hank stood, opened an overhead cupboard and pulled out a can of ground coffee. "I've restocked the kitchen. I'm going to have a bowl of soup and coffee for lunch. Kinda like hanging around sometimes. You hungry?"

"I could eat."

Hank dug in a drawer and pulled out a can opener. "Williams tells me your partner's got four legs and your sour disposition. What's the story there? You still having trouble getting someone to appreciate your going-for-broke style?"

"Don't even try to look innocent." Sunni ignored Mac's warning growl and snatched the scrap of silk from between his big hairy paws. "You and your partner are—"

"We're what?"

Sunni whirled around to find Jackson standing in her bedroom doorway. His gaze traveled to the red thong she held, then to where Mac sprawled in the middle of her bed among some of her most colorful naughties.

"He raided my dresser." The explanation wasn't necessary. Anyone with half a brain could see what had kept Mac occupied for the past hour. "He's a pervert. He's—"

"Got good taste."

"I should have expected you'd take his side in this. Well, that's fine. He's out of here, and so are you!"

Sunni tried to stay calm, but that was impossible. Jackson had been gone all day doing God knew what, and she had been stuck in her apartment with a psychotic mutt who couldn't stay out of trouble if you bribed him with two steaks and a ham bone every ten minutes.

"My red bra, the one that matches these—" Sunni waved her panties like a flag "—I think he's eaten it. That bra was seventy-five dollars, my cost."

"So I guess you've had a bad day."

Sunni's gray eyes narrowed into slits. "He ate two silk pillows, and my Portland rose bush has gone to plant heaven. And after all that, I still watched the Westminster Dog Show with him for two hours. I've gone over and above, and this is my reward."

Hands on her hips, she waited for Jackson to say something. Instead, he shoved away from the doorjamb and sauntered to the bed looking too good for words. First he picked up a sheer black bra off the bed, then a sin-sizzler red garter belt that was wet with dog drool.

Sunni eyed the garter belt, minus one garter. "He's ruined at least a thousand dollars' worth of silk in less than an hour. He's either chewed, snagged or drooled on everything that came out of that drawer."

"At least he's not wearing something. That's a relief. His shrink warned me that I should expect anything."

"His shrink?"

"Mac's in recovery." He handed her the soggy garter belt. "Would a woman my mother's age wear this?"

"Not in the shape it's in now." Sunni glared at him, then snatched the garter belt. He didn't let go right away, not until the elastic was stretched between them. In that *strained* moment their eyes locked, and again the heat that had been circulating between them for the past two days sucked her throat dry. Sunni tossed the garter belt and the thong into the open drawer Mac had pilfered. "What do you mean he's in recovery?"

"He lost his partner a few years ago. After that he was sent to the K-9 pound to wait to be reassigned. Only, the partners that teamed him couldn't get along with him."

"What a surprise," Sunni mocked. "I do wonder why."

"It really was a surprise. Mac was their top K-9. The theory is that he lost too much all at once. He lost his partner and his partner's wife in a matter of days. The shrink thinks he couldn't handle losing them both and that's why he shut down."

The story made Sunni take a longer look at Mac

where he lay sprawled among her silk. "Why do you suppose they did that?"

"Did what?"

"Why did they strip him of everything familiar to him? Wasn't losing his partner traumatic enough? I don't understand."

"Nate Taylor's wife contested the decision to take Mac from her, but she lost on the grounds that K-9's are police property."

"I think that's terrible."

"Terrible enough to forgive Mac for making this mess?"

"The Portland rose bush was—"

"A one-of-a-kind?"

"No. One of my favorites." Sunni sent her eyes down the length of Jackson's body, another favorite thing she was into these days—feasting her eyes and letting her imagination wander. She watched him shrug out of his jacket, studied his soft cotton gray shirt, remembering what was underneath.

"I talked to the cab driver. He pretty much saw what you saw."

"That's good, right?"

"It confirms that the car deliberately sideswiped you. Is that good? No."

"Meaning?"

"Meaning, we're moving in permanently."

"Excuse me?"

He walked to her closet and opened it. Pushing her silk aside, he hung up his jacket. "You heard me." He turned around, his gaze locking with hers once more. "Me and Mac are your new roommates until this case is wrapped up."

For the past two days she'd resorted to injecting

her morning insulin into her thigh behind that closet door. If that continued, what were the odds she'd be discovered? Sunni shook her head. "You can't."

"Can't? We've been here for two days, and we've been doing fine so far, right?"

"Wrong."

He glanced at Mac, who had decided to stretch out with his nose inside the cup of one of her bras. "Okay, so I'll keep a better eye on him. But we—"

"But nothing." Sunni's lips suddenly started to tingle. It was clearly a warning that she needed to check her blood sugar. All day she'd been feeling a bit off. See, this was why he couldn't move in. Her stress level was screwing up her sugar level. She needed peace and quiet, and she needed her privacy.

Aware she had to do something, she turned to her nightstand and pulled open the second drawer. As casually as she could, she picked up a bottle of pain relievers and pretended to extract one. As she placed the bottle back in the drawer, she curled her fingers around a sugar cube, then closed the drawer. Her back to him, she popped the cube into her mouth, pretending it was the head pill.

"Got a headache?"

Stuffing the sweet sugar into the side of her cheek, she turned to face him. "Are you surprised?"

"I'll replace the pillows. And I'll buy you another rose bush. As far as Mac goes—"

"No. My apartment will look like a hovel within twenty-four hours if he stays here. I'm sorry his *recovery* is slow, but the Wilchard is going to have to be close enough…for both of you." Sunni glanced at the clock. Fifteen minutes and she'd start to feel better. Or would she? She had the sudden urge to giggle.

Horrified, she grabbed Jackson's arm and propelled him toward the door. "Mac, come on. Out."

Mac jumped off the bed and trotted into the hall. Jackson cleared the door and stopped. "Sis, you all right? You look—"

"Exhausted. Who wouldn't baby-sitting a kleptomaniac? Go."

"And do what?"

Sunni reached for the door and started to close it. "Something. Anything. Nothing. I don't care, as long as you do it out there instead of in here."

He started to go, then stopped again. "How's your back? You look like you're moving better."

"Better. Yes…much better. Go."

"I'll start dinner."

"No, start packing." She slammed the door shut and locked it. A second later, the pile of silk on the bed was on the floor, and Sunni was sprawled on the comforter sucking on two sugar cubes at one time and holding a roll of Life Savers.

Chapter 9

"What are you doing out here?" Jackson stood in the doorway of Sunni's greenhouse and watched her snip at a large potted rose bush at the end of her worktable with a pair of silver garden shears. Around and above her hung baskets of roses in a dozen different colors. They were pretty and smelled good, but he knew for a fact that nothing and no one smelled better than Sunni Blais.

He knew because he'd been sleeping with her right under his nose for two nights and her exotic scent had been permanently burned into his memory.

"What's going on, Sis? You've been quiet all evening. You didn't say two words at the kitchen table. What's the matter, you don't like steak?"

"It was very good."

"Wine too dry? Next time I go shopping, want to come along?"

She kept working with her back to him, the scissors

making fast little snipping noises. Something was definitely bothering her, and Jackson intended to find out what it was. If she was still angry with him for refusing to move out, they were going to have to come to some kind of an understanding, because he wasn't going to gamble with her life a second time.

She turned, her face as serious as he'd ever seen it. She had on a slippery silk dress—another supersoft nut buster. It was open at the neck and short sleeved—a garden party of colors on a white background. Shorter than her work skirts, it showed off more leg above the knees than her father would have approved of.

The dress was free-moving…loose. It would be easy to get underneath. Yeah, that's what he'd thought about the minute he'd seen her come out of the bedroom wearing it, when he'd knocked on her door and told her that dinner was ready.

And while they sat across from each other at the table, he'd kept wondering what color her panties were, or if they covered her perfect backside. His lusty thoughts had turned him stone hard and he'd stayed that way throughout dinner.

He was still hard an hour later.

"You didn't need to buy groceries."

"The coffee supply was getting low. You know me and my morning coffee. Your juice, too. And with us moving in—"

"This isn't going to work."

"Sure it will, Sis. Something will open up with the case before long."

"That's not what I'm talking about and you know it."

That look said it all. They'd been dancing all

night—side-stepping each other in the kitchen, trying to clean up the table and dirty dishes without touching each other. She'd caught him staring at her more than once, and he'd caught her doing the same.

The truth was, he wanted to get it on with her and she knew it. And just maybe she wanted to get it on with him, too. He had mixed emotions about that. She was the boss's daughter, and for both their sakes he'd hoped that his hard-on disgusted her. That if he got too close, she'd drive the point home with her knee—sometimes what a man needed most was a direct blow to the area that was causing him the most trouble and overriding his good judgment. And right now what he wanted most was to get his hands underneath that loose-fitting dress.

"You're staring, Jack—"

"And liking what I see."

She hung the shears on a hook, then lifted the plant off the table and put it back in its place. "I think you should go watch TV or, better yet, pack up your stuff and—"

"You know I can't do that."

She leaned against the table, resting her hands on either side of her hips. She gave him a brazen shake-down that took in all of him, her eyes unblinking when they settled on his crotch.

"That's right, Sis. I'm wearing my feelings tonight. It's not news, though, is it?"

Her mouth parted and she exhaled a breathy sigh. "No, it's not news."

Jackson took one step into the greenhouse. "It looks as if I'm not the only one displaying his feelings tonight. The twins are putting on quite a show."

"You think it's because of you?"

''You saying different? Saying it's the chilly night air? Could be. It's cool tonight.'' He took another step toward her. ''It would be for the best if that was the case. Say it, Sis. Tell me it's the night air and I'll head for the shower. That way we'll save ourselves from making a serious mistake.''

''And that's what it would be? A mistake?''

''Pretty much.''

She drew her lower lip into her mouth and closed her eyes. She was doing battle with the situation, weighing the *mistake.*

Jackson swore, then took the last three steps. She had to have heard him, had to have felt his heat—the temperature in the greenhouse had tripled in a minute's time. But she didn't open her eyes, didn't stop sucking on her lower lip.

He covered her hands where they gripped the edge of the table on either side of her and leaned in.

''Jack...''

He dipped his head and boldly inhaled her special scent, deliberately brushing his cheek against hers. ''I like how you smell.'' He gently pushed her head back by hooking his nose beneath her chin. Her head fell back, offering him her throat. Jackson felt like attacking her, moving in fast and taking everything all at once. But he also wanted to savor the moment, to listen and watch her reaction to everything he did to her.

He brushed his lips over her neck where her pulse beat wildly, then trailed kisses to her collarbone. He felt her shudder and it energized him. Slowly he moved back up her neck, kissing an inch at a time. When he reached her ear, he changed course and outlined her delicate jaw with more of the same.

"Jack," she said again, her voice shaky.

"How 'bout it, Sis? We gonna get to know each other better? Or are you gonna put me in my place pretty quick before it's too late?"

He stepped back and waited for her eyes to open. When they blinked open and her head moved back to look at him, she said, "And if I was going to put you in your place, Jack, how would I do that?"

"Your knee moving upward oughta take care of it."

"And if I decided we should get to know each other better?"

He studied her face, her sultry gray eyes. "Either way, it's your move."

"Let my hands go, Jack."

Jackson released her hands, unsure what was going to come next. Likely her knee, hard and fast. Way to go, fool, he chastised himself. Give her the ammo, then just stand there and let her fire away.

He waited, braced himself the best he could for a frontal attack, only it came from a different direction. Instead of bringing her knee up, she straightened and stepped around him. She circled him twice, stopping behind him the second time.

"What are you doing, Sis?"

"Moving. Isn't that what you said I should do, make my move?" She came around him once more, and this time she was smiling. "I don't think I've ever seen you sweat, Jack. You hot?"

"You know I'm burning up."

"I've been watching you for days, Jack. Looking you over from all angles."

"That makes two of us."

"Yes, I know."

"And?"

"And I really do like looking at you, Jack."

"Me, I'm partial to touching. Maybe we can incorporate the two."

"Maybe."

She circled him once more, and she was still smiling when she landed in front of him again. Unable to keep up the verbal game without getting his hands in on the action, Jackson clasped her around the waist, lifted her off her feet and set her on the end of the worktable. Face-to-face, his hands settled on her thighs. Slowly, his fingers turned inward and spread her legs wide. He stepped into the open vee a moment later. "This is a change," he said huskily. "Me between your legs instead of the other way around."

Their eyes locked.

Time lagged.

She leaned forward and settled her hands on his chest, stared at his mouth. "In case you're wondering, Jack, I'm making my move. Is it too subtle?"

He grinned, his arms sliding around her, one hand going high, the other low. The high one popped the clip that held her hair off her neck, and her shiny black hair tumbled around her face. The low hand urged her hips forward slightly so her open thighs brushed his. Then he was kissing her, eating at her mouth, licking her lips, nipping her chin. He heard her sigh, felt her shiver. He took her sweet breath into his mouth and then gave it back to her in an even hotter kiss.

Her hands were no longer flat on his chest, but working open the buttons on his shirt. He stopped kissing her long enough to pull his shirt free of his jeans, then watched as her hands shoved the edges wide.

She closed her eyes as her fingers threaded through the hair on his chest. She moaned softly, her tiny fingers flexing and stroking, as if touching him had been some kind of long-awaited hungry need she'd been wrestling with in private. The idea undid him. He'd never experienced anything like the feelings that were suddenly storming his insides.

He leaned forward and kissed her, peeled her dress off her shoulders and let it fall to her waist. "Hell, Sis," he groaned, then dipped his head and kissed the swell of each ripe naked breast.

"Jack..."

In short order, his hands followed his mouth, adoring her firm, hot flesh, plucking at her nipples with his fingers and stroking the underside of each breast. He moved the heels of his hands along her rib cage and curved his fingers around her fullness. Drawing her breasts together, he dropped his head and sank his face into her sweet flesh. "Smother me, please," he breathed into her deep cleavage, enjoying the sweet scent of her and the sound of her moaning in pleasure. In answer, he used his tongue and teeth to drive her further over the edge—licked and nipped and suckled until each rosy nipple was a solid stone.

She arched her back in silent approval, sending a surge of hungry heat straight into Jackson's groin. His hands found the hem of her dress and he slid it up her thighs, slipped his fingers underneath.

She lay back on the table, her body anxious, her eyes closed. He shoved up her dress, exposed her slender thighs and virgin-white panties. His hands slid beneath her, rewarded with the feel of warm flesh.

The knowledge made him groan as he cupped her bare bottom and lowered his mouth to her quivering flat stomach. His hot breath moved over her as his lips adored her. He circled her navel, then dipped his tongue inside.

Her hips lifted, and she whimpered. In answer, he moved his mouth lower and kissed her mons through her tiny thong. The gesture had her crying out and lifting her hips off the table. ''Easy, baby,'' Jackson whispered, dropping his head to taste more of her.

She was moaning and panting when his cell phone rang. The crazy musical sound it made bounced off the walls of the greenhouse like a fire alarm. He released her and straightened, his gaze locking on her passion-glazed eyes, then on her heaving breasts.

The phone set off again. He swore, then reached into his pocket and retrieved it. As he continued to stare at her, he flipped it open, checked his own breathing, then said, ''Ward here.''

''I thought you were going to e-mail me today.''

Clide. Jackson watched Sunni draw her lower lip into her mouth, her cheeks as rosy as her aroused taut nipples.

''The day's not over yet.''

''Damn close. I'm suppose to be asleep within the hour. That nurse I've got carries a pitchfork, along with her stethoscope. I swear she works for the devil. If I'm not asleep in twenty minutes, she'll be back in here to raise some hell.''

''Nothing news-breaking to report. Go to sleep and I'll e-mail you in the morning.'' Jackson still hadn't broken eye contact with Sunni. She hadn't moved, not an inch, her dress still bunched at her waist, the dark curls between her thighs visible beneath her white panties.

"So, where you at? My baby girl safe from the wolves tonight? You doing your job protecting her from those unconscionable bastards? You ain't laying down on the job, are you?"

Clide's words struck Jackson between the eyes, then kicked him in the gut. Then in the ass. He reacted by backing up and turning his back on Sunni. He said, "She's fine, Chief. Safe from the wolves."

"How's Mac doing? Is he worth feeding, or will you be looking for a new partner once you get back?"

"He's coming around."

"Hell, I think I hear that she-devil with the pitchfork coming. Don't forget to e-mail me in the morning."

When the phone went dead, Jackson slid it back in his pocket, then turned to find Sunni standing, her dress back on her shoulders and her thighs covered.

"My father?"

Jackson nodded. "Listen, that call was fate giving us both a reality check. Your father's timing—"

"Stinks."

Jackson swore, then shot a hand through his hair. "I'm here to clean up a mess, not make an even bigger one."

She said nothing, just stared at him.

"Come on, Sis. Help me out here." He jammed his hands in his pockets in case he lost his head and tried to touch her again.

Her nose hiked a notch and her pretty gray eyes narrowed. "News flash, Jack. If you would have had the balls to put me back on that table you would have found out that I'm a no-mess, no-strings, no-promises kind of girl. And you would have had the ride of your life. A free ride."

"Meaning?"

"Meaning I wouldn't have expected anything in the morning."

Her confession surprised him. He hadn't expected it, or considered that maybe all she had wanted tonight was some good old-fashioned hot sex.

I'm a no-mess, no-strings, no-promises kind of girl.

Her words should have made him feel relieved. Most men liked no strings, and got tongued-tied making promises.

The ride of your life. A free ride.

No man in his right mind would turn down a free ride, especially a free ride from Sunni Blais. But he was going to turn it down, because for the first time in his life he wanted more from a woman than just hot sex—more from Sunni Blais.

"I'm going to take a cold shower and clear my head. And since your back is on the mend, I'll make a bed on the sofa. Good night."

The lavender tile beneath her bare feet felt cool, the humid air warm on her shoulders. Sunni closed the bathroom door behind her and stepped farther into the room, her gaze settling on the shower where the tangled lovers etched on glass clung to each other. But she was no longer interested in phantom lovers and fairy-tale dreams. She wanted a real lover—no, not any lover, she wanted the man standing naked beneath the pulsing shower spray.

She wanted Jack.

His eyes were closed, the shower spray bouncing off his chest and naked thighs—off his hips and marvelous butt. Sliding down his long, rock-hard hairy legs.

She watched him raise his arms and send his dark stubborn hair away from his forehead. The muscles in his shoulders bunched and the veins stood out. She licked her lips as several rivulets raced down his flat stomach and into the nest of dark hair surrounding his perfect "package."

He hadn't cooled off much from his aroused state in the greenhouse. No, not much...

Sunni was in the process of shrugging her dress off one shoulder when he opened his eyes. Her hand froze on the silk clinging to her breasts as his green eyes nailed her where she stood. She hesitated only a second, then shoved the dress to her waist, past her slender hips. The silk pooled at her feet, and she stood in her white thong and nothing else.

A long minute ticked by, then the shower door opened, Jackson's long, hairy arm splayed along its width. It was clearly an invitation, and Sunni didn't realize she'd been holding her breath until that fact had been confirmed.

Without a word, three steps brought her to the door. His gaze shifted to her naked breasts, and to break the tension, she said as she stepped inside the shower, "The answer is yes, Jack, it's all me. No implants or hormones." Her gaze traveled to that area of him that set him apart from the general male population in a *big* way. "How about you? Taking hormone shots?"

Boldly he followed her interest to gaze at himself. "What you see is the real deal, Sis. That, and a little more, if you can handle it."

"Handling it would be my pleasure, Jack."

His gaze found hers, and without breaking it, Sunni

pulled the door closed behind her. When he just stood there staring, she stepped forward, backed him up and pressed herself against the full length of him. "What is it, Jack? Am I too much, too fast? Or are you all show and no action?"

Baiting him was dangerous, but Sunni wanted his hands on her, the way they had been on her in the greenhouse—all over every inch of her.

"Do you know what you're asking for?"

"Do I look confused?" Sunni opened her hand to allow him to see what she held before placing the small square package in the tiled cove built into the shower wall.

He still hadn't touched her, hadn't raised his arms. Sunni rubbed her breasts over his hard stomach, and when she heard him moan, she stepped back and licked water beads off his nipples, fueling the fire. "Turn me down, Jack," she taunted. "Send the boss's daughter away."

She moved her hands to his hips, then bent her knees to trail kisses down the center of his chest as she had imagined doing in her dreams for the past two nights.

Around his navel.

Lower.

He made a guttural moan a moment later, his hands moving forward and his fingers tangling in her wet hair to hold her head.

"Look up, Jack," Sunni instructed, then opened her mouth to taste him.

"Hell, Sis," he moaned as she began to torture him. "What am I going to do with you?"

"What do you want to do with me, Jack?" Her

hands touched him. Stroked him. Her mouth adored him.

"Everything. Every damn thing," he groaned.

Sunni remembered how he had looked at her standing in the doorway of the greenhouse. Needing to see that same hunger in his eyes now, she backed off and looked at the ceiling mirror. Finding his gaze, she said, "Then what are you waiting for? I'm on my knees already, Jack, but if you'd like to hear me beg—"

"What I'd like—" his arms suddenly captured her waist and dragged her up his body "—is to taste every inch of you."

Sunni shivered as he walked her backward into the water spray. There, he kissed her with enough hungry heat to knock the air out of her lungs. Dizzy, she clung to him as his hands moved possessively over her slick body. When his lips followed his hands and he tasted her breasts, Sunni arched for him, eager to feel his mouth on her flesh.

Suddenly he was turning her around and rubbing himself against her bottom. His arms curled around her, his hands cupping her breasts as he nipped at her neck and gyrated his hips. Then he was on his knees, kissing her bottom, peeling her panties off her hips and sliding them down her legs.

"Face me, Sis."

When she turned, he was standing again. He kissed her once more, then reached for her wrists and raised her arms over her head to secure her hands around the gold fixture. As he bent his knees and squatted, Sunni knew what was coming next, and she gripped the fixture to keep her balance.

The sound of the water spray faded as her mind

and every nerve ending in her body became attuned to Jack's lips and tongue on her flesh. The heat from his mouth and the roughness of his hands drove her crazy. Her knees grew weak and her body shook. She knew she was going to come apart soon.

"Jack..."

He must have heard the need that was choking her. The torture eased up, and she opened her eyes to find him standing in front of her. His hand snatched the little square package off the shelf, and she watched as he slipped the condom on. His gaze found hers a moment later. "You look like you need rescuing, Sis. Lucky for you there's a cop close by."

He flashed her a wolf's grin as he reached up and took her hands off the shower fixture and placed them around his neck. Lifting her, he urged her to wrap her legs around him. His eyes were bright and watchful as he slid halfway inside her. Sunni sucked in her breath, but she didn't close her eyes. She wanted to see his face, watch and remember.

"You all right?"

He didn't move deeper, and she knew why. Without warning, she snatched his lower lip and bit down hard enough to get his attention, but not hard enough to cause him pain. When she let go, she said, "No holding back, Jack. I know I'm tight. And I know you know what that means."

He didn't say anything for several seconds. Then he smiled. "Hungry, Sis?"

"That's right, Jack. I'll take everything that's on the menu...please."

Chapter 10

"I'm not taking Mac to work with me. So stop harping on the subject."

Jackson tossed another dish in the dishwasher. "I have some things to check out today. I don't have a choice."

"So check them out."

She was being stubborn, but she had no idea that he had given definition to the word. "Either take Mac with you or stay home." He dried his hands on the dishcloth dangling from the waistband of his jeans and turned around. "After the cab incident—"

"What are you staring at?"

"Are you all right? You look—"

"You're suppose to say I look beautiful the morning after, Jack. Be careful."

"You always look beautiful, Sis. You also look tired. You don't have to go to work today. You could—"

"I'm fine, Jack. Perfect, as a matter of fact."

He'd sent her into four climaxes before midnight. Another two after that. She'd had two glasses of orange juice this morning, and was sipping her third as she came toward him from the bedroom. But like she'd done all morning, she was avoiding his eyes.

"Should we talk?" he asked. "Discuss last night?"

"Of course not. What are we going to discuss? Who moaned the loudest?"

"You did." His baiting to get her to look at him fell through.

Once she'd fallen asleep in his arms he'd lain awake and watched her. She was so damn beautiful, and he was in so much trouble.

Think of her as a member of your family, Ward. The old cliché, guard her with your life, works for me. If it don't for you, imagine there's a crazy police chief holding a gun to the back of your head ready to blow it off the minute you screw up.

Well he'd screwed up all right. Up, down, backward, sideways. Standing up, lying down.

"Did you hear me, Jack?"

"What?"

"Why does Mac keep staring? And he's been following me everywhere since I got up this morning."

"He's got the hots for you. I think that's why he went crazy at Silks the other day. I think he could smell you, but he couldn't find you and it drove him nuts."

"And that's why he's not coming with me today. I don't need him going nuts again."

She tracked past him back to the bedroom, Mac on her heels. Jackson pulled the dishcloth from his jeans and walked into the hall. "You're going to be in the office, right?"

"Yes," she shouted.

"Then I don't see a problem. If he stays with you, he'll be happy."

She came back into the hall with a scowl on her face. Finally she met his gaze. "But I won't be happy, Jack. No. He's not coming with me."

His gaze swept over her. "God, you're perfect."

"No one's perfect, Jack. Perfection is an illusion. Everyone has flaws. Even you."

"Name one."

"You smoke too much."

"Not lately."

"No, not lately. So what does that mean?"

He wasn't ready to advertise that he'd quit smoking just yet. Maybe because he didn't quite believe it himself. But, yes, he'd virtually quit smoking cold-turkey after twelve years of living on three packs a day. He knew that was unheard of, and yet it had happened.

"Jack?"

"I don't know. You've been keeping my hands too busy, I guess." He reached out and wiggled his fingers in the direction of the twins. "Want to be late for work?"

"I'm already late." She headed past him. "Thanks for breakfast."

He trailed her. "All I get for eggs Benedict is a quick thanks?"

She turned, sighed, then leaned forward and touched his lips with a chaste kiss minus the trimmings. "There. Thank you."

"Why do I get the feeling you're thanking me for more than just breakfast? And that by noon you and

I will be back to dancing around each other? What's wrong, Sis?''

''Jack, please. I—''

He reached out and hauled her up against him. ''Look at me, dammit.''

She did, and what he saw in her eyes confused him. She looked afraid. ''Jack...''

He kissed her gently. She was shaking. ''What's wrong, baby?''

''Nothing.''

''Prove it. Kiss me like I know you can kiss,'' he challenged.

''Jack...''

''I'm not going to let you go until I know tonight we won't be dancing. Unless it's cheek to cheek,'' he teased.

''I guess you just wore me out last night,'' she confessed. ''But it was wonderful. Every...inch.'' Then to prove her words, she kissed him—kissed him with all the trimmings.

The kiss promised that she hadn't gotten her fill of him yet. Good, Jackson thought, because it would take him forever, and long after that, to get his fill of Sunni Blais.

When she was about to pull away, he tightened his hold on her and offered back what she'd given him. The kiss dragged on, and still he was reluctant to let her go. Finally, he set her away from him. ''Mac's going with you. And you don't have to take a cab. Joe's limo is waiting for you out front. I'll be at Silks to pick you up at five-thirty. Don't leave the building.''

''No Mac. But I'll agree to the limo. See you at five-thirty.''

Jackson let go of her. She didn't look back as she left. Through the peephole he watched her standing at the elevator in her silk suit. She looked good in red. She looked better naked, moaning and saying his name as if he were her savior.

When the arrow above the elevator blinked, he opened the apartment door and sent Mac on his way. Sunni stepped inside the elevator, and seconds later—quick as a mouse—Mac slipped in alongside of her.

On the twenty-fifth of each month, exactly at two o'clock, Tomas Masado entered Silks wearing the same scowl and the same black leather jacket. It was a routine that had been established almost immediately after Sunni had opened Silks two years ago.

She was at the sales counter speaking with Mary when he came through the front door. They made eye contact, he motioned to her office, then headed in that direction.

He disappeared behind the door just as Sunni remembered Mac. "Oh, no! Mary, this will have to wait." She scrambled around the counter, and as she approached her office, she could hear Tomas swearing behind the door. She glanced over her shoulder, hoping her customers were too busy to hear, then dashed behind the door just as Mac sent the city's toughest bad boy up on her desk.

"Mac, no!"

The dog stopped advancing at the sound of her voice, but he continued to bare his teeth. Sunni hurried forward and pulled him back, then laid her hand on his wide head and patted him. "It's all right."

Lucky climbed off her desk. "He would be dead

if I hadn't been concerned with splattering his brains around your office.''

''Well that's visual, Lucky. Don't you get tired of always playing the Terminator?''

''Lucky?''

Sunni's cheeks turned warm, but she didn't explain how she knew his nickname. ''I have the packages. They're right here.'' She moved to retrieve Frank Masado's order from the credenza along the wall behind her desk. Mac followed.

''So Jacky thinks you need a guard dog these days, does he?''

She turned, holding a beautifully wrapped package. ''Jacky?''

''We all earned nicknames years ago. Joey was Joe Cool 'cause he liked to wear sunglasses. Jacky got his nickname from watching *Jacky Challenger,* a Saturday morning cartoon.''

This was the most Lucky had said to her in the two years Sunni had known him. Surprised by his sudden willingness to speak, and fascinated by the topic of conversation, she prompted, ''Then you've known Jack…son for a long time.''

''Forever, I guess. Vina used to put up with me and Joey hanging around on a daily basis. We practically lived there.''

''Vina?''

''Lavina Ward, Jacky's ma. She sorta adopted us after my mother died. She's got a picture of all three of us kids on the wall at Caponelli's. We're sitting on her couch. Jacky's got me on his lap. Hell, he and Joey can't be six. Me… I think I'm still wearing a diaper.''

The revealing monologue must have surprised him. Suddenly Lucky looked extremely uncomfortable. Which had to be a first, Sunni decided. Most of the time he was bulldozer bold, and always in a hurry.

He shrugged, glanced around the room. "God, I wonder where the hell all that came from?"

Sunni refused to feed his embarrassment with a comment. Instead, she stepped forward and handed him the packages. "Tell your father the two gifts inside are exactly what he ordered. No substitutes this time."

Lucky nodded, then his gaze traveled to Mac. "If Jacky thinks you need the dog, keep him close. He's got good instincts and he's smart. But I didn't say that, all right? If he knew I was proud of him, he'd hold it over my head. He don't always play fair."

"Do you?"

"What's that?"

"Do you play fair, Lucky?"

"Pretty much. I'm an eye-for-an-eye kind of guy." He reached in the pocket of his black leather jacket and checked the list he always carried—Frank's do list, was what he had once called it. "I guess he wants pink next time. See you next month."

Jackson met Hank Mallory at Tom's house at three in the afternoon. That morning, he'd checked out a lead on Elizabeth Carpenter that had turned out to be a dead end. As he stepped inside the kitchen he could smell fresh-brewed coffee.

"I heard you drive up. Thought you might need a cup of caffeine."

Hank looked like he was in a better mood today.

Jackson accepted the cup of coffee and headed for the table.

"You look tired. Up all night?"

Jackson didn't answer, but in a roundabout way he had been *up* all night. Only he'd told Sunni days ago that he didn't kiss and tell, and he didn't. What they had shared behind closed doors would remain their private affair. "I just checked out another false lead where Elizabeth Carpenter is concerned. I've been thinking, what if she wrote that letter?" He took a swig of black coffee. "What if she was working with the killer?"

"Her reason would be?" Hank sat across from Jackson and cradled his own coffee cup.

"She was an addict. Addicts need money."

"She was getting paid for her dancing."

"But was it enough?" Jackson scratched his head. "It's like she just vanished. Maybe she cleared out of town."

"If you're right about her working for the killer, it would have been a smart thing to do. Disappear, that is. You play with fire, you get burned. Trust me, I know."

Jackson studied his ex-boss, his last comment making him uneasy. "You got something you want to get off your chest, Hank?"

He looked up. "Me? No."

"*Trust me, I know.* What do you know?"

"Oh, that." He shrugged. "Nothing. Just thinking about the job and how explosive it is on so many levels. That's all."

Not entirely satisfied with his answer but willing to let it go for now, Jackson said, "I think Elizabeth Carpenter got a job at Silks just to steal Sunni's silk scarves. We already know she worked at the Shedd and that she lied about that. I learned from Sunni that Elizabeth paid a visit to her at the apartment one evening, which establishes opportunity. She's also been identified by three desk clerks at the Crown Plaza as the pretty blonde on Milo's arm when they entered the elevator on a number of occasions. The night Milo was killed, she didn't show up at the Shedd. And that's odd, because I'm told she never missed."

"You've made a lot of headway in a short time."

"Not enough."

Hank sat back and grinned. "You're a helluva good detective, Jackson. I've missed you and your talent." He stood and refilled their coffee cups. "Has Sunni Blais confided in you? Are you sure she's not hiding some dark secret? No surprises in her closet?"

"She's not hiding anything." Jackson spoke the words with confidence. He had spied on Sunni for five days, lived with her for four. He knew what was in her fridge and how she liked her eggs. And he knew what she liked best in bed, too—what would make her shiver and moan and come apart in his arms.

No, she wasn't living a double life. He would know it if she had a secret.

Jackson was still musing when his cell phone rang. He flipped it open quickly. "Yeah."

"Say Ward, it's Stud. I just got a call you might be interested in. We've got a female sleeper recovered from a car that was pulled from Diversey Harbor late morning. If it's the Carpenter woman, it looks like we got us another body. 'Course I'm not sure it's her. If you're interested—"

"I'm interested. I'll meet you downtown." Jackson

disconnected and shoved to his feet. "Could be Elizabeth Carpenter just surfaced."

"Dead or alive?"

"Dead." Jackson headed for the back door. "She was found inside a car in Diversey Harbor. I'll call you when I find out the facts."

"We'll be closing in an hour."

Sunni looked up to see Mary had poked her head into her office. "Is it that late already?" She glanced at the crystal clock on her desk. "Oh, I guess it is."

The telephone rang.

"I'll get it, Mary."

As Mary closed the door, Sunni reached for the phone and lifted the receiver to her ear. "Silks Inc., Sunni speaking."

"You alone?"

"Jack?"

"You alone?"

"Yes. No. Mac is here beside me."

"Right answer, Sis. He been behaving himself today?"

"He's been a perfect gentleman."

"I guess our talk must have done some good. How about you? You been behaving?"

Sunni loved Jack's heavy voice. It could actually produce chills and carnal images. "I've been behaving. Just what was it you two talked about?"

"Keeping our number-one girl happy."

"Well, Mac's done his part today. What do you have planned to put a smile on my face?"

There was a definite pause before he said, "You ever made love on the top of that desk you're sitting at?"

Sunni's gaze swept the length of hardwood in front of her. "No."

"Want to?"

"Jack..."

"Want to?"

"...yes." Another chill attacked Sunni's body and she squeezed her eyes shut. Jack was taking over her body, as well as her every waking thought. That wasn't supposed to happen. She'd just wanted one night. One night in his strong, very capable arms. One memory. But this morning she hadn't wanted to climb out of bed. She'd wanted to stay and make another memory, and then another.

"You still there, Sis?"

"I'm here. And where are you? You said you'd meet me here at five-thirty."

"That's why I'm calling. I'm going to be a little late. I got a lead on Elizabeth Carpenter. Can you sit tight and wait for me?"

"Yes."

"No more than an hour. Okay?"

"I'll wait. I've got a ton of paperwork to catch up on. Two days' worth to be exact."

"You needed the time off."

"I'm not sorry." Sunni knew he understood her comment held a double meaning.

"I'm not sorry, either."

Sunni glanced down to see Mac's head had found her lap. Stroking his head, she said, "I'll see you later, then."

"Yeah. I have a key. I'll let myself in."

Sunni hung up the phone and soon found herself daydreaming. The minutes ticked by slowly. Mary came and went at five-thirty. She ate a small box of raisins for a snack, knowing that dinner would be late. Especially if Jack made good on his earlier proposition.

She stared at her desk and imagined lying naked on the smooth surface with Jack just as naked. The image made her throat go dry, and she began to clean up the papers that were scattered.

At six o'clock Mac stood and faced the door. Sunni smiled and decided Jack had gotten his work done sooner than he expected. She stood when Mac trotted to the door. She didn't notice the hair rise on his back until she opened it and he shot out ahead of her and started barking.

That was her first warning that something was wrong. The second was that instead of heading for the front door, Mac raced toward the hall that led to the storage room and bathroom. Suddenly a door slammed, then Mac's bark took on a more frantic pitch.

Fear tangled in Sunni's throat as she stood in the darkness among the silk racks. She waited several minutes, uncertain what to do, her heart hammering inside her chest.

Another door slammed, and she nearly jumped out of her skin. Mac's barking turned more frantic, and the fear for his safety suddenly overrode everything else.

She headed back into her office and snatched up the crystal paperweight that sat on her desk. Back in the showroom, she realized that she was perspiring heavily, her anxiety full blown. She reached the small hall moments later and could see in the darkness that the storage room's door was open.

There could be a simple explanation for that, she

told herself. Mary could have forgotten to close it—they were in and out of that door a dozen times a day. Nonetheless, Sunni gripped the paperweight tighter and forced herself to keep going, too afraid to turn back for Mac's sake.

She crept past the bathroom. Entered the dark storage room. There was another separate room, a huge walk-in-closet she used to hang back-stock. The door was closed and it was obvious that Mac was inside.

Sunni touched the wall beside her to get her bearings. Remembering where the light switch was, she reached out to flick it on, only instead of touching the wall her hand came in contact with a warm, hard body. She screamed and jumped back, but not before the body lunged at her.

She raised the paperweight and swung hard. It made contact with a sickening thud. Encouraged, she drew back to swing again, but this time the paperweight was knocked away and she was shoved hard into the opposite wall with such force she felt the air whoosh out of her lungs.

She gasped for air and tried to stay on her feet. Mac was going crazy inside the closet now. If she could only get to him, she thought. If only she could get the door open…

An iron hand locked around her arm and pulled her away from the wall, then hurled her into a wooden shelf. This time Sunni screamed, her knees buckling to send her to the floor. Dazed, she lay on her side unmoving. Knowing that someone was looming over her, she closed her eyes and waited for a solid blow to come, waited for the worst. But it wasn't pain she felt seconds later, it was a smooth, leather-gloved hand stroking her cheek.

Sunni wanted to fight the hand, to fight to stay awake. Only she couldn't move, couldn't fight the dizziness that broadsided her in waves, keeping her paralyzed and helpless.

Twenty minutes later, she slipped into unconsciousness.

Jackson strode into the lobby at Masado Towers fifteen minutes later than he wanted to. His mood was sour and his jaw set, his mind on the difficult task of telling Sunni that Elizabeth Carpenter had been found in a rental car that had been missing for as long as Milo Tandi had been dead.

He crossed the little stone bridge as he pulled Silks' key from his pocket. He unlocked the door, stepped inside and, in the act of relocking the door, heard the noise. The door forgotten, he spun around and scanned the darkness, his Diamondback .38 already in his hand.

The light from Sunni's office drew his attention first and he headed for the room, all his senses honed razor sharp. Outside the open door, he stuck close to the wall, the .38 cocked and ready for a confrontation.

He went in fast, but there was no one inside. No signs of a struggle. No blood.

He let out a sigh of relief, then left the office and followed the noise to the back of the shop. He entered the hall and found the door where the noise was coming from. He eased open the door and crept inside, identifying the noise as wood splintering. *Mac…*

He kept his back against the wall as he moved forward, his free hand sliding ahead in search of a light switch. He found it seconds later and—his gun at the ready—flipped the switch.

The sight of Sunni lying lifeless on her side three feet away nearly dropped him to his knees. Jackson had never come apart on the job. He'd learned early on that to be a good homicide detective there was no room for wasted emotions. Action is what saved lives—that, and crystal-clear thinking. But emotion was climbing all over him as he knelt beside Sunni's limp body. "Oh...no, Sis."

His throat closed off, his heart broke open.

On instinct his shaking fingers settled on her neck. As pale as she was, he never expected to find a pulse. But the minute he did, all of his skill and expertise surged forward.

Within seconds an ambulance was on its way and Jackson was assessing Sunni's injuries—none of which looked serious enough to cause unconsciousness.

Chapter 11

She was a diabetic.

An invisible knife took Jackson's wind as if the expensive Hibben that rode his hip had been unsheathed and buried deep into his chest. As many times as he said the word, he still couldn't believe it, couldn't believe she'd tricked him so completely.

He stared down at Sunni lying in the hospital bed, and again the ordeal he'd walked in on at Silks a few hours ago chilled him to the bone. Yes, someone had made an attempt on her life, that was his fault. But if he had known she was a diabetic he would have…

What would he have done?

He turned away from the bed to stare out the third-story window. A moment later, the same dozen questions that had been attacking him for the past two hours revisited him. How could this be happening? Why hadn't she told him? Why hadn't Clide? How could he have missed the signs?

Hell, the signs had been there—the orange juice she consumed by the gallon. The snacks he'd found in the drawers in the bedroom…

"Jack…"

Her husky voice made him jump. He hadn't expected it to be so strong. He turned and found her sitting up. When he didn't say anything, she glanced around the room, then tossed the white sheet aside.

"No, don't get up. The doctor's keeping you here until morning for observation."

"That's ridiculous. I feel fine."

"But you're not fine…are you?"

His sharp tone made her flinch. "Okay, Jack. So you know I'm a diabetic. My secret is finally out."

Secret… The word stung him, and in reaction, he grunted, then turned back to the window.

"Jack? I bottomed out, okay? It happens. Not to me very often, but—"

He spun around. "If I had gotten there ten minutes later you would be dead right now. Dead!" His loud, angry voice bounced off the walls.

"Are you blaming that on my diabetes, or the creep that attacked me in the storage room?"

"Dammit, don't be cute. Dead is dead. You know what I'm talking about."

"I know I could have died, yes. But I didn't."

"You should have told me you were a diabetic. I would have definitely done my job differently had I known you were a walking time bomb."

"A time bomb? I have diabetes, Jack, not some horrible disease."

"Who's been feeding you that lie? You got a tooth fairy for a doctor? News flash, baby, diabetes *is* a disease. The number one death-causing *disease* in the country."

He wanted to hurt her. Wanted to punish her for tricking him into thinking he'd been doing his job a hundred percent. And he wanted to hurt her for playing with his emotions, too.

She'd misrepresented herself, dammit, and he would never have allowed himself to care as much as he did if…

Jackson tried to rein in his temper, but his pain was colored by anger and it was too close to the surface. "Oh, yeah, you have a disease," he taunted. "A disease that'll most likely kill you someday. Probably sooner than you think if you keep taking chances like you've been doing lately."

His cruel words sent the color draining from her face as if he'd just slit her throat. "All right, Jack, have it your way. I have a *disease.* I'm going to *die.* So…now that we've got that settled, where's Mac? Is he all right?"

The tears that shimmered in her eyes never fell. Jackson felt like scum. No, he *was* scum. He wanted to take the words back, wanted to go to her and hold her. He wanted to tell her he was sorry. Sorry she was sick. Sorry that he'd been late. So damn sorry.

He said, "Mac's spending the night at the vet's. He has a pound of wood between his teeth. When I got there, he'd nearly eaten through the door. He's scheduled for minor surgery in the morning."

"But he's going to be all right?"

"He isn't going to feel like brushing his teeth for a few days, but he's a survivor. Were you ever going to tell me?"

The question had her looking away.

Jackson swore, shook his head, then laughed bitterly. "I told you once before, lying makes messes messier."

"You don't understand."

"Baby, you can't begin to know how much I understand."

She jerked her head back to look at him. "Meaning?"

He should tell her about his father, but he wasn't going to. What was the point? "Meaning, if I had known you were a diabetic, I would have—"

"Kicked me out of the shower? Is that what you would have done, Jack? Having regrets already?"

Regrets. How could he regret sleeping with the most beautiful woman in the city? The sex between them had been mind numbing and completely over the top. He'd never experienced anything like it. No other woman even came close to what he had shared with Sunni last night. No other woman had made him shake one minute and soar like a rocket the next. No other woman had kept him up all night, unable to get his fill of her. And when he'd worn her out, he'd lain awake for hours just watching her and touching her.

It was just a damn good thing he hadn't gotten carried away and spoken out loud what he'd been thinking and feeling. They had known each other barely a week. No promises had been made. He was in town to do a job—keep her alive while he found Milo's killer. His agenda was still the same.

"This afternoon Elizabeth Carpenter's body was recovered from Diversey Harbor."

"She's dead. Oh, no."

"I think it's likely she was killed by the same guy who killed Milo. Probably the same person who showed up at Silks tonight. Can you give me a description of your attacker?''

''It was dark. I couldn't see. But I did hit him with the paperweight from my desk. I heard him grunt, so I know I hurt him. I think it was a man because the noise he made was low and rough. He was also very strong and wore gloves. He lifted me and tossed me like I weighed nothing at all. He was taller than me, but not as tall as you. Did you call my father?''

''No. But I will. He's—''

''Don't.''

''Why?''

''My parents don't know. They don't know I have diabetes.''

Her admission shocked him. ''They don't know?''

''I wanted the time to be right. I wanted… I don't know what I wanted. Maybe not to have to tell them at all.''

Jackson swore. ''How could you keep something this damn important from them? They deserve to know.''

''Don't you think I know that? They're coming for the Christmas holidays. That's when I had planned to tell them. That's when I *will* tell them. But not now. Please, Jack.''

''Sick people need someone to take care of them.''

''I'm not sick. I don't need a nursemaid. I'm capable of taking care of myself.''

''Didn't look too capable lying on that storage room floor tonight, white as a ghost.''

''That's a cheap shot, Jack.''

''I think it, I say it. Remember?'' He pulled on his jacket.

"Jack, wait. Promise me you won't call my father."

"There's a guard outside the door, compliments of the CPD. He'll be there all night. As far as your father's concerned, I'll sleep on it and let you know what I decide in the morning."

A brisk knock on the door sent Jackson to answer it. When he swung it open he was surprised to see it was Joe. "What are you doing here?"

"I came to see the prettiest lady in the hospital," he said. "She awake?"

"She's awake."

Jackson stepped aside and watched his friend walk into the room carrying a dozen yellow roses in a cut-glass vase. "Did I come at a bad time?"

"No." Both Jackson and Sunni spoke at the same time.

Joey's black eyebrows arched as he studied first Jackson, then Sunni. Finally he set the roses on the metal table next to the bed, then took Sunni's hand. "You all right?"

"Yes."

"I just wanted to come by and—"

"Show your concern?" she inserted.

"I'm your alibi, remember?"

"Did you make sure Detective Williams saw you?" She glanced at the roses. "They're beautiful, Joey. Thank you."

"Persian yellows. Hard to find. I called all over. Well, my secretary called all over. As far as Detective Williams is concerned, he missed my entrance. But I'm sure my coming and going will be documented by the guard out front. It'll keep our alibi story solid."

Jackson saw Joe wink at Sunni, and a moment later the vision of his friend kissing Sunni on the terrace revisited him with detailed clarity. He headed for the door. "I'll be back in the morning to take you home. Doctor said not before eleven."

"Jacky, wait up. How about a cup of coffee?"

Jackson paused, his hand on the doorknob. "I don't feel like coffee right now."

"Come on. There's a coffee shop downstairs."

"If we're going to talk and drink, it won't be coffee and it won't be in a sick-house that smells like antiseptic and death. You want to talk, meet me at the Shedd. I got business there."

"Okay." Joey touched Sunni's cheek. "You take it easy and get some rest."

Jackson watched her nod, watched her gaze find him over Joe's shoulder. He opted to say nothing. Everything between them had pretty much been said.

"She's not sick like your father, Jacky. There's no similarities."

Jackson sat at a corner table in the main lounge at the Shedd. The smoke-filled room was making him hungry for a cigarette, but the two half-naked, blond dancers on the glitzy, lit-up runway didn't interest him in the least. "Is that why you showed up at the hospital?"

"I like Sunni. I want her safe," Joey supplied. "It made sense to show up bearing gifts to keep the alibi story looking legit."

"So that was it?"

Joey shrugged. "When I heard what had happened at Silks I thought maybe you might need to talk."

Jackson snorted. "Talk about what?"

"This is me, Jacky. We played a lot of games as kids, but not twenty questions. That night at Caponelli's, when I first saw you, all you could see was Sunni Blais. Struck by lightning is what it reminded me of. The next day in my office you tried too hard not to let your feelings show. Lucky noticed it, too. And then tonight Sunni confirmed my suspicions. That look she gave you..." Joey whistled. "That, friend, was one powerful look. If I'm wrong, say so, but ten to one, you two are past business and polite conversation."

"I don't want to talk about it." Jackson reached for his beer and tipped his head back, draining half the bottle before he set it down.

"Okay, then just listen. I talked to Sunni's doctor. She's in good health. No kidney or heart problems. No vision problems, so far. No visible signs she'll have long-term problems until she's so old it won't matter. Your old man, on the other hand, had one foot in the grave before you were born. He was half blind by the time he was Sunni's age. He couldn't hold down a job, or take a leak by himself. Remember? We used to get him up, each of us on either side of him and take him to the john."

Jackson made no comment, he simply stared at beer bottle number three.

"I'll say it again, Jacky. Sunni's not sick, not like your old man was."

Jackson lifted the bottle to his lips again. He wanted to get drunk. Needed to get drunk. He drained the beer, then flagged the waitress for a refill. "You sound like you're trying to sell me a high-risk bad investment, Joe. I'm heading south as soon as this case is wrapped up, remember? Why should I care that the boss's daughter has health problems?''

''Out of sight, out of mind?'' Joey shook his head. ''It don't work that way, Jacky. Not if she's gotten under your skin. And I say she's burrowed clean through.''

''You sound like you're speaking from experience.'' Jackson studied Joe's eyes. ''Is that why you never got married when you were supposed to? Did someone *get under your skin,* bro? Is that why you called off the wedding to Sophia D'Lano? You never really said why.''

''Have you heard something I should know about?''

Jackson shook his head. ''No. Just a hunch. This mystery woman must have been really something for you to chance all-out war with Vinnie D'Lano. What his daughter wants, his daughter gets.''

''I don't love her, Jacky, but she fits into the family plans. Frank's worried his sons aren't going to marry and make baby sons for the organization. You know, the sons are the future.''

''So do you plan to marry Sophia D'Lano?''

Joey shrugged. ''I've been stalling, that's true. I can't much longer.''

''I hear a *but* in there. Is there someone else?''

''No. Not any longer. But I have regrets, Jacky. Too little, too late, as they say. But if I had stood up to that saintly bastard and gone after what I wanted three years ago, I wouldn't be sleeping alone right now.''

''Joe Masado sleeps alone? We can't be talking about the same Joe Cool I used to know?''

''You haven't looked at that runway once, friend.

That's not the Jacky I used to know. That's why I'm telling you, that out of sight doesn't mean out of mind."

Jackson scowled, not liking his words tossed back in his face. "Okay, Joe. Bottom line. I care about Sunni, but knowing what I do now, I'll probably run like hell when this case is over."

"I think that's the beer talking."

"I never came back to Chicago planning on staying. This just makes it easier to accept the Louisiana heat." Jackson took a long pull on his beer, then flagged the waitress once more.

"Got any new information on the case?"

"The Carpenter woman is dead. She was found this morning." Jackson shook his head. "She didn't nosedive that car into the harbor by partying. We both know that, Joe."

"So what's next?"

"I need to force this guy out into the open. Make him make a move. The wrong move."

"Got a plan?"

"Maybe. But to make it work, I'll need to call in a favor." Jackson leveled his friend *the look*.

"What do you need, bro?" Joey grinned. "Just ask and I'll see if I can deliver."

Jackson settled back in his chair and rested his arm on the table. "What I need is someone crazy enough to do something illegal for me. Know anyone who qualifies?"

Joey's grin spread.

Seconds later, Jackson cracked a smile. It was obvious that they both had the same *crazy* in mind. He asked, "Think he'll do it?"

"If you ask nice."

After Jackson had detailed the plan, he waited for Joe to comment.

"It's risky."

"I'll tell him you said that. Tell him you tried to talk me out of asking. I'll say you don't think he's up to it."

Joey chuckled. "Getting him mad used to work when we were kids. He used to turn into a hailstorm on wheels." That said, he raised his bottle. "To the old days, Jacky."

Jackson raised his fifth bottle of beer. "And to the hailstorm on wheels."

"Jackson, why on earth are you sitting in the dark?" Lavina Ward stood in the doorway of her kitchen after flicking on the light. "Did you tell me you were going to come over? I don't remember you saying—"

"No. I didn't say I was coming by, Ma. Sorry it's so late." Jackson shoved himself slowly to his feet. He'd been sitting in the window seat that overlooked the backyard. He had a headache from too much beer and breathing in too much smoke without tasting it.

"Business good tonight?"

"A full house," Lavina offered. "Coffee?"

"Yeah, I could use some."

"I agree. I can smell you from clean over here." She got busy in the kitchen. "So why didn't you tell me that Mac was a dog? I had to hear that from Crammer Ferguson at the supermarket. And he was downright smug about it once he saw I had no idea what he was talking about."

"You still gonna cook him a six-course meal?"

"Was there a reason for not telling me your partner was a dog?"

"Maybe at first I was a little sour about the idea of having a four-legged partner. But not anymore. I guess you could say we're a good match." Jackson staggered into the kitchen to stand over his mother's shoulder.

She looked back. "Need a lesson in brewing coffee or a shoulder to lean on? You're about as pale as a wash rag. Not going to pass out, are you?"

"No."

"Need an ashtray?"

"No, I quit."

"You quit? Praise be! When did that happen?"

"A few days ago."

"So you're here to talk. Is that it?"

"I guess."

"At the table, or out on the back step? The night air might do you some good. For sure it'll make you smell better."

"The table's closer, and not so low to the ground. Once I get down I might not get up again." Rubbing the back of his neck, he turned and headed for the table.

"So where's your partner now?"

"Spending the night at the vet's."

"The vet's?"

"He's having gum surgery. Decided to eat a door."

"A door? Are you serious?"

"It's a fact."

His mother finished pouring the water into the coffeemaker, then turned around and stared at him from across the counter. "Okay, let's hear it. You don't do stupid things, Jackson. So what's this all about? Is something wrong with Joe or Lucky?"

He shook his head. "No. She's got diabetes, Ma."

He hadn't meant to blurt it out like that. He'd come to talk about it, but he'd planned on easing into it.

"Who has diabetes, Jackson?"

"Sunni Blais." He made a swipe through his hair, feeling sick all over again. He wished he had a cigarette. He'd definitely quit smoking too damn soon.

"Why don't you explain?"

"That's what I'm doing, Ma."

"Back up and give me a little more information, son."

His mother's voice had softened. He nodded. "Okay, from the beginning." By the time he had finished bringing his mother up to date on the case, she'd poured coffee twice into their cups.

"That poor girl. An insulin reaction, at the same time she was being attacked by some crazy killer. To survive all that she must be tougher than she looks."

Jackson raised both eyebrows and scowled. "A week ago you were calling her dangerous, Ma. Now she's a tough girl?"

"Maybe I spoke too hastily. She sounds like she's someone I'd like to get to know. A lot of the diabetics I visit at the medical center are bitter. Some take my words of encouragement, but so many don't and believe they're either being punished, or that they'll never live a normal life. Sunni sounds like she's determined to rise above her illness."

His mother still belonged to a support group for diabetics and their families. Jackson thought she should give it up, but she had told him that her experience was meant to be shared, and if she could help just one person by offering support, then it was worth it.

"Jackson, if you got drunk over this, what does that mean, exactly?"

He stood and began to pace while his mother watched him wear out her rugs. "It means I would have appreciated a little honesty from her. I'm out busting my ass to keep her safe and she… I can't do my job if I don't know the bottom line."

"So it's doing your job that's got you angry?"

"Hell, yes, it's the job. Keeping her alive is why I'm here, Ma."

"What does her father say? I'm surprised he didn't give you all of the facts before he sent you here. Did he tell you why he didn't share that information with you?"

Jackson snorted, then stopped pacing. "Because he doesn't know. She's been keeping her little secret from everyone. Even her folks."

"Oh, dear. When did you say she was diagnosed?"

"Two years ago."

"Something must have happened."

"What do you mean?"

Lavina sipped her coffee. "Usually if they hide their condition it could mean that they're not able to accept the illness themselves, or someone else hasn't been supportive. Acceptance can be just as hard for family and friends as it often is for the diabetic. You know that. You had an awful time at first. Blaming your father for being sick all the time."

"Ma, just lay it right out there."

"You were young. You didn't understand."

You don't understand.

You have a disease. A disease that'll most likely kill you. Sooner than you think.

He caught his mother studying him as if she were going to pickle him and was deciding which end to start with. "Okay, let's hear it. Why are you swimming in guilt? What did you say to that poor girl to make her feel worse and you run for the bar?"

His mother's words knotted Jackson's gut. "She should have told me."

His mother's brows pleated. "So you told her off, then went out drinking." It wasn't a question.

"I went out drinking because I felt like it, Ma."

"You went out drinking 'cause you feel guilty over something and you're angry. Angry at yourself."

His mother knew him too well. "She should have told me, dammit! Before I—"

"Before you what? You've known this woman a little over a week. Are you... Have you... Oh, dear."

He walked to the window and stared out at the stars.

"You care about her, then? That's what this is about?"

Jackson didn't answer.

"You care, but you don't want to care. Especially now that she's going to require a little more work."

"Dammit, Ma, sink the knife in a little deeper."

"If you had no clue she was a diabetic, then she can't be all that sick. She owns a business. That requires a healthy mind and a body to go along with it. We're both in agreement that she's beautiful and intelligent. There are different types of diabetes, Jackson. Did you talk to her doctor?"

"She's IDDM."

"Okay, so she uses insulin. Thousands of people

do. Correction, the smart people do. That's good news. That means she's taking care of herself.''

''Complications can crop up overnight, Ma. Dad—''

''Harold had major problems, Jackson. The day we met and fell in love, I knew our life together would be short. Actually, your father outlived the doctor's time line.''

Jackson stared at the clubhouse, with its weathered slat board and chipped white paint. The clubhouse had been his escape as a boy, Joe and Lucky his salvation. His mother was right; as a kid he'd been bitter about his father being sick all the time. But then things had changed. His father had won him over with his steadfast faith and gentle heart. They had loved hard and fast in those last few years and not one minute of life had been wasted on anger or regret.

''Jackson, you can't run from your feelings.''

''That's what Joe said.''

''You've talked to Joey about this?''

''Yeah.''

''Good.''

''She's a diabetic, Ma.'' Jackson faced his mother. ''I feel helpless.''

Lavina set her jaw. ''What makes you think you're above dealing with a little bad along with the good? Why should the person you care about be required to be in perfect health as well as beautiful?''

''I never said she had to be perfect.''

''Good, because you're far from it. But healthy, right? You want to care about Sunni, but only if she's in perfect health?''

Jackson had thought if anyone would understand it would be his mother.

"I can read your thoughts. The only regret I have is that Harold is gone. But I never regretted one day of loving him. The good outweighed the bad. You may find that hard to believe, but every day I reached out and touched his face while he slept, felt his breath on my hand, I thanked God that he had given Harold Ward one more day. The truth is, I believe he put Harold in my life, just like he put Sunni in yours. Life isn't based on coincidence, Jackson. Now," Lavina pointed to the chair across from her, "sit and tell me what you said to Sunni in the hospital. The very first thing."

Jackson ambled forward and sat. "I don't remember."

"I imagine you asked her why she lied to you."

"I guess."

"It always makes things easier if you put the blame on others. But it's your problem if you can't deal with her illness, Jackson, not hers for having it."

"Whose side are you on, Ma?"

"Yours. But when you're wrong, I'm not going to pat your head and tell you, good boy. I didn't coddle you as a child and I won't do it now that you're grown."

"I'm whining without cause. Is that it?"

"No, you have cause. And whining has its place. It cleans out the cobwebs clouding the brain so you can think clearly and admit the real reason why you had one too many beers tonight."

"And why was that, Ma?"

"Out of fear. You're afraid to love and lose. But think of this. You're a homicide detective, Jackson. You probably have a greater chance of getting yourself killed than Sunni does dying of diabetes."

Before Jackson could comment, his cell phone rang. He pulled it from his jacket pocket and flipped it open. "Ward here."

"It's done. I got everything you asked for. It's waiting for you at the location you specified. And those eyes and ears you were expecting just pulled up out front. I'll stay here until you show. When do you think that'll be?"

"I'll be there in twenty minutes." Jackson stood and jammed the phone back into his pocket. "I've got to go, Ma."

"Jackson, does she know how you feel? Does she know you love her?"

"I never said I loved her."

Lavina sighed, shook her head, then rose and went to the cupboard. She retrieved a bottle of pain relievers, rolled two into her hand, then tracked back to the table. "Here. Take these and chase them down with the rest of your coffee. Drive with the window down. It'll blow the stink off you and clear the rest of the cobwebs still clouding your brain. Hopefully, by the time you get to where you're going, you'll be thinking straight."

Chapter 12

Lucky was waiting on the back porch of Tom Mallory's house nursing a bottle of Scotch, when Jackson walked up the sidewalk. He was glad he'd taken his mother's advice and driven with the window down on the way over—he was thinking more clearly than he had been a half hour ago.

"Right on time," Lucky said, then tipped up the expensive bottle of Macallan.

"You get everything I asked for?"

"It's all here. Everything."

Jackson glanced at the door. "Joe inside?"

"He was. Frank summoned him. And you know what that means. *Subito. Presto...presto.*"

Yes, Jackson knew what that meant. When Frank snapped his fingers he expected his boys to jump. "You go see Crammer Ferguson?"

"I did. Gave him the extra hundred like you said and sent a message to Hugh Egan to get his plumbing crew over there pronto. Water will be running by tomorrow.''

''Threaten Egan's life if he didn't jump, or did you give him a visual?''

Lucky grinned. ''Funny thing about rumors, Jacky. They always make out the bad guy to be meaner and more heartless than he really is. And likewise, the cop out to be a saint. But you and I know there's good and bad on both sides.'' He shrugged. ''But, what the hell, sometimes the rumors can be a blessing. My reputation has been carrying me further than my fists these days. Damn good thing, too. Some days I move pretty slow.''

''Get rid of the bottle, bro. You'll heal quicker.''

''You sound like Joey. Yeah, I've been thinking about it.'' Lucky shoved to his feet, then hitched his free hand in his back pocket. ''We'll talk when I get back.''

''Get back?''

''I'm taking a quick trip. I know the timing stinks, but this can't wait. We're square, right? You got what you need from me?''

''If you brought me everything on the list, I got what I need.''

Lucky grinned. ''Saw to it personally.''

''No one saw you? You're sure?''

''No one.'' Lucky came off the porch a step at a time, moving slow, verifying his admission that he wasn't a hundred percent healthy. Once he walked past Jackson, he took one step off the sidewalk and poured the last third of the Scotch into the grass. ''See you when I get back, Jacky.'' He started down the sidewalk, the neck of the empty bottle clasped in his scarred hand. Suddenly he stopped and looked over his shoulder. "I put a few of my men on notice that you might call. Left their names with Joey. Need some muscle at your back, use 'em. Don't want to get a call from Vina that you got yourself killed. I left you a present in the broom closet. Later, *mio fratello.*"

"Later, bro."

Jackson climbed the steps and entered the kitchen. Glancing around, he noticed the bags of groceries Lucky had brought. He put them away, then brewed a pot of coffee. Suddenly he remembered the broom closet, and he opened it to find Lucky's *lupara* standing in the corner. The deadly Sicilian shotgun was outfitted with a leather holster that was studded with ammo.

Grinning, he closed the door, then checked his watch. It was late—well after midnight. He headed for the stairs that led to the second story, not bothering to turn on any lights—he knew Tom's house as well as he knew his own apartment back in New Orleans. He also knew where to find the light inside the bedroom at the top of the stairs. But the light was already on when he reached the room, the door open by half. He shoved it wider, then stepped inside.

He had thought she would be asleep by now. The plan had been to check on her and leave. Only Sunni was wide awake, wearing black pants and a lavender silk blouse, sitting in a small rocker near the window. Her hair was loose and soft around her face, her eyes alert.

"You should be in bed by now," he told her. "Officially you're not supposed to be out of the hospital until tomorrow, remember?"

"You could have told me I was going to be kidnapped. My heart almost stopped before I realized it was Lucky who had slipped into my room. I don't know how he got past the guards, but—''

''I didn't ask. It's best that way. Knowing how when it comes to Lucky can only bring on a powerful headache or turn your stomach inside out. But he never fails to get the job done. That's why he's always the go-to guy.''

''You should have told me what to expect.''

Jackson shrugged. ''I didn't come up with the idea to spring you until after I left the hospital. The fewer people who know where you are, the better. I don't trust anyone at this point.''

''No one except Joey and Lucky Masado.''

''That's right. As hard as it is for most people to believe, they're good guys. They just don't wear white hats.''

''Lucky told me you grew up sharing the same neighborhood.''

Jackson nodded. ''We grew up sharing the same everything. They're the brothers I never had, and Vina and me are the family they couldn't buy no matter how rich their daddy was. Did Lucky bring you what you'll need to be comfortable for a few days?''

''You mean did he pack my insulin? Yes.''

''Good.'' Jackson sent his eyes around the room, then curiosity had him open the closet. Inside he found a black silk robe, a few colorful silk blouses, a skirt and two pairs of jeans. He'd never seen her in jeans, but the idea of her small backside outlined in denim sent a surge of heat into his groin.

''I called your father.'' He heard her swear, and he closed the door and turned. ''No, I didn't share your secret with him, or that you were attacked tonight.

But I did tell him that I was moving you out of your apartment for a few days. I also told him about Elizabeth Carpenter."

"You're sure you didn't mention I was a diabetic?"

"No."

She stood, and her sure movements confirmed what the doctor had told him—Sunni hadn't been injured by her attacker. Still, he needed to make sure. "You feeling okay?"

"I feel fine."

She certainly looked fine. Better than fine, really. That's why he hadn't considered she might be ill. He would never have guessed.

He headed for the hall. "Lucky stocked the kitchen cupboards, and the bathroom. You should have everything you need."

"Whose place is this?"

Jackson stopped in the doorway. "It's Tom Mallory's house. A cop I partnered a few years ago."

"Is he away on vacation?"

"No. He's dead."

"Oh."

"He was shot and killed off duty."

"Did it happen three years ago?"

"Yes."

She stood and walked to the closet. A moment later the black silk robe was tossed to the bed. His gaze fell on the silk, then tracked back to Sunni. She turned around and was sizing him up in much the same way he had been doing to her since he'd stepped inside the bedroom. "I thought you were leaving."

"I was. I am... Listen, at the hospital I was—"

''Forget it, Jack. You think it, you say it. That's what I like about you. No bull.''

Jackson winced inwardly. ''I was—''

''Being honest. You really did say it best. Diabetes is a disease and someday I'll die from it. That's the bottom line.''

How could he have said that to her? What kind of a monster was he? ''Sis, that's not really true, you know. The medical field has made some remarkable advancements in—''

''Cold hard facts, Jack. That's what I'm interested in. Actually, I have you to thank for bringing me back to earth. Things are much clearer now, and that's good.''

He needed to apologize, needed to explain to her why he'd taken the coward's way out earlier and lashed out at her. His mother was right—out of his own fear, he'd attacked the one person he would cut his arm off to keep safe and make happy. ''Sunni, I want to—''

''It's late, Jack, and I'm tired.''

He nodded, watched her turn her back. A moment later her silk blouse slid off her shoulders. He stared at her smooth, flawless back, her delicate spine and narrow waist. There were no visible signs that she wore a bra. He let out the dammed-up air inside his chest and said, ''I want you to call Mary tomorrow and tell her you'll be off work for a couple of days. Joe agreed to keep an eye on Silks for you. Hank Mallory's offered round-the-clock protection out front on the street. No one gets in or out of the house who isn't on the list I gave him. I'll be on the couch if you need something. The bathroom is—''

She turned around clutching her blouse to the

twins, pushing them up so that the creamy swell teased his eyes and sent another voltaic charge of heat into his groin. "I know where everything is. Lucky gave me a tour. Good night, Jack."

Sunni opened the fridge and stared at two gallons of orange juice. She had woken up hungry minutes ago and it had driven her downstairs. It was the middle of the night, but hungry was hungry.

She'd slipped out of bed and crept down the stairs as quietly as a gnat. The living room was off to the left and she'd entered the kitchen without disturbing Jackson's sleep.

She took one of the gallons of orange juice from the fridge, and by the small light on the stove, poured a glassful, then returned the gallon to the fridge. Sipping the juice, she raided the cupboard and munched a handful of peanuts. She had just set the juice glass in the sink when she sensed she wasn't alone.

She turned slowly to find Jackson leaning against the doorjamb. He had definitely been sleeping—his hair was tousled, his chest and feet were bare. His jeans were riding low on his hips and his zipper was half hitched.

"What's going on, Sis?"

She should hate him for the cruel words he'd said to her at the hospital, but he'd been right. And he'd also been justified in delivering the *cold hard fact* in an angry voice and with fury in his eyes. Still, she wouldn't let him slice her to bits a second time. And the safest way to prevent that from happening was to keep at least a good ten feet between them. Better yet, excuse herself and make a quick exit back upstairs.

''I was hungry.'' She refused to give him more information than was necessary.

''Want me to fix you something hot?''

''No. I found what I needed, thank you. I'm on my way back to bed.''

He didn't move.

''I'm sorry I woke you. Go back to bed.''

He shoved away from the door frame and came toward her. ''Now that I'm up, I'm *up*.''

His blunt words sent Sunni's eyes to his crotch. And it was true, he was *up*. He walked past her and poured himself a cup of cold coffee from the old stuff sitting in the coffeemaker.

Seeing her chance to escape, she headed for the door. But she wasn't quick enough—he reached out and grabbed her wrist, then took a swig of coffee and made a face. ''That's bad.''

''It's late, Jack. I'm talked out.''

''Me, too.''

Slowly, he drew her toward him. Sunni angled her head. ''Sex, then, that's what you want? Should I keep my eyes closed so I don't have to see the disgust in your eyes, or do you have a blindfold for me?''

''I could never be disgusted by you. You torture me, Sis. That's what you're seeing in my eyes.'' That said, he locked his hands around her waist and lifted her onto the counter in a single motion. ''We didn't get a chance to try out your office desk. Ever do it in a kitchen?''

His husky voice sent shivers up Sunni's spine, but she needed to fight them, to fight… Jack. She was too vulnerable where he was concerned.

''You smell good. Feel good.'' Fingers splayed, he slid them over her stomach to her thighs.

"Jack, please put me down."

His fingers curled inward and slowly spread her thighs open. "You liked me touching you last night."

"Last night we were equals. Tonight I have a disease and I'm dying, remember? And since you've learned that *fact,* you've been staring at me as if you expect it to happen any minute."

He stepped into the open vee of her legs. "I was upset. I said things I had no right saying. But I thought you trusted me. Then the next thing I know I'm learning you have a secret. I'm learning you have..."

"I have what, Jack? You can't even say it without getting the word caught in your throat. Let me go."

"No." Suddenly his hands were in her hair, peeling it away from her face, his gaze practically smoldering with heat as he looked into her eyes. "If you catch me staring, I'm remembering things. Things we've done. Things we haven't done. Things I want to do to you...with you."

He kissed her mouth without the slightest hesitation, the heat driving Sunni's mouth open and her eyes closed. She loved his warm mouth, his gentle hands. His lips trailed her throat, then moved lower, his breath dancing over her breasts, his nose nudging them as he boldly inhaled her scent. She felt his tongue tease one of her vulnerable nipples through her robe. When he had the little nub hard and the black silk wet from his attention, he moved on to the next nipple.

"Jack..."

"I'm right here."

His hands parted her robe to expose the black chemise she'd worn to bed. His fingers brushed the dark curls between her legs, once. Twice. "No panties. Oh, baby..."

She heard the air whoosh out of his mouth, and she let out her own held breath and his name along with it.

"I want to watch a solo performance on the counter," he whispered against her lips.

He was suggesting he make love to her with his hands and watch her come apart. His erotic words made her shiver as his palm flattened out and slid over her mons.

His name was caught on a tortured moan as he parted her and two fingers sank inside.

"My fingers feel good, don't they? Ride my fingers, baby. Come on. I know you want to."

He moved his thumb forward and stroked slowly. He knew what he was doing, where to go, how fast to move, how hard to push. What would make her the most vulnerable. What to do to her to make her *his*.

"Jack..."

Sunni came apart in front of his eyes hard and fast. Her body moved against his loving fingers—magic fingers—with a sudden need so strong she soared swiftly and violently. Proudly and openly.

He'd once told her she wore her feelings. Tonight there was no doubt she'd exposed her soul, driven by the euphoria that she was fast realizing always came when she was in Jack's arms, surrendering to his unrelenting touch.

His lips were warm as he kissed her seconds later, drawing her lips into his mouth like savored pieces of candy. When his tongue came, it teased and coaxed at first, then turned into a hot poker—probing and searching. Hungry and determined.

He had the most marvelous breath, Sunni thought, as his tongue entered her mouth like a dragon breathing liquid fire. She moaned softly, felt his hands shove the straps of her chemise off her shoulders along with her robe. As he peeled the silk from her breasts he broke the kiss to watch them spill forward. ''So damn beautiful,'' he sighed, then bent his knees and kissed each ripe swell, tugging on her nipples with his lips, then nudging them with his nose and gently torturing them with his unshaven chin. His mouth back on hers, he whispered, ''I want in... inside you.''

''Jack, no. Stop...''

He stood slowly, his gaze sweeping her swollen lips, then her tortured nipples. Sunni's breath hitched in her throat and she knew he heard it. That's why he wasn't backing off, why he hadn't stepped out of the notch between her legs. His hand went to his back pocket, produced a wrapped condom. ''Is that a firm *stop,* or just a wait-a-minute-let-me-catch-my-breath kinda *stop?*''

The question hung in the silence. One minute dragged into two.

''That's what I thought.'' He took her hand and laid it against his zipper. Sunni hesitated only a second before her fingers found the metal clasp. When her hands slipped inside his jeans, he said, ''Push 'em down. Free me up.''

She pushed his jeans off his hips, and as he urged her to wrap her legs around him, she bent her knees. He half lifted, half dragged her forward off the counter, and then, in one smooth solid motion, he was inside her.

Sunni gasped in surprise, then again as he bucked his hips forward and sank deeper into her tight sheath.

He was so hot, and so incredibly hard…

Sweet agony was what came to mind as Sunni clung to his sturdy shoulders, each thrust of his hips taking them closer to a mind-numbing, earth-shattering climax.

They were both slick with sweat when surrender joined them in replete moans of victory. Seconds later, he was kissing her as deeply as he was seated, the air around them ripe with the spicy tang of spent passion.

Sunni buried her face against Jack's neck and tried to catch her breath—tried to rationalize what had just happened. What seemed to always happen when they gave into this powerful sexual attraction they had for each other.

But there was no rationalizing pure ecstasy, Sunni thought. Or how or when she'd fallen so desperately in love with Jack.

"You asleep, Sis?"

Sunni was holding on to him for dear life, too shattered in both body and mind to speak.

"Sis? You all right?"

"Just catching my breath." Slowly, she leaned back and looked at the man who had become so important to her in such a short time. "That was…"

"Fast," he breathed heavily, studying her face. "Should we try it a little slower…upstairs?"

Sunni woke before dawn and slipped out of bed. Quietly, she wrapped her robe around her nakedness, then went downstairs to the bathroom. After she'd given herself her insulin injection, she slipped back upstairs, removed her robe and eased back into bed to curl up next to Jackson's hot body.

"Everything all right?"

Eyes closed, Sunni snuggled close. "Yes. Go back to sleep."

She felt him shift his body, the bed creaking more than it would have over a minor adjustment. She opened her eyes to find him on his side, his arm stretched out high on the pillow. "What are you doing?"

His fingers began to play with her hair. "Touching and watching. My two favorite things to do when I'm with you."

Sunni slid her hand up his chest, her fingers sliding through the soft dark hair to curl around the silver cross that he wore. The cross had three distinct crossbars. She'd never seen him without it. "And what do you think about when you're touching and watching me, Jack?"

"Lately?"

"Yes, lately."

"Mostly I think you don't look sick."

His answer was unexpected. "What does that mean, exactly?"

"It means you look good. Better than good." He offered a small smile. "That's why it was such a shock when the paramedic said your unconsciousness last night was brought on by hypoglycemia."

"And you knew what that meant right away?"

He nodded. "But you're not sick. Not like my dad, anyway. Joe's right. There're no similarities except for—"

"Excuse me? Your dad's a diabetic?"

"Was. Diagnosed at age six. Dead at forty-eight."

His unexpected declaration hit Sunni like a hard fist to her stomach. She moaned inwardly, tried to keep from wearing her emotions, and sat up slowly. She kept her face averted as she attempted to escape the bed. Her heart was suddenly pounding wildly and there was a rushing noise in her ears.

Jackson reached out and tugged her back down beside him. When she tried to push him away, he leaned over her and pinned her to the mattress with his chest. "What's wrong?"

"I—nothing."

He tossed the sheet back over both of them, then rested his arm along her side and curled his fingers around her upper arm. "I acted like an ass last night at the hospital. I'm not trying to excuse it, just explain."

"I haven't asked for an explanation, Jack. Really, I... I don't want one." Sunni closed her eyes, fighting tears.

He kissed her. "Open your eyes, sweet thing." When she did, he said, "My dad's diabetes was acute. He had advanced heart problems before age twenty and wasn't expected to live to thirty. He married my mother when he was twenty-nine against the advice of his family and the doctors, but—"

"Jack, I don't need an explanation. I—"

"Ssh... Let me get this out. I was born four years later. Dad never worked a day of his life. My mother opened Caponelli's to support us, and while she was at work I took care of him. I ran bedpans, gave him insulin injections...cooked. Wiped his nose, and the other end, too. There were days at a time when I lived at the hospital. I used to hate it so much that... Well, I used to...is all."

"Jack, let me up."

"Ssh... The first thing I thought about last night when I learned you were a diabetic was...oh, hell, this can't be happening. Not again."

"Jack, please."

"That's why I was angry. Why I—"

"Okay, Jack! I get it." She shoved hard, and when he let her go, Sunni scrambled off the bed and quickly pulled on her robe. "I don't recall asking you to be my nursemaid, Jack. It sounds like you've had plenty of practice, but I'm not ready to climb into bed and die just yet."

"What the hell are you talking about?"

Sometimes honesty wasn't the best policy, Sunni thought. But then again, Jack's you-think-it-you-say-it policy had certainly brought her head out of the clouds and settled her feet firmly back on the ground...once more.

Last night she'd been so afraid that the look in his eyes had been disgust. Now she knew it hadn't been disgust at all. What she'd seen was pity.

Oh, God! She'd been such a fool.

"Come on, Sis. Talk to me. Why are you looking at me like that? You're mad. Why?"

How dare he paint such a horrible picture, then ask her why she was mad. "You want me to talk. Well, here it is, Jack. I know what I am, but it's my problem. Mine. I'm not asking you to share any of it, so you can breathe easy. I'm the free ride, remember? No mess, no strings, no promises. And that's the way I want it. So don't worry. You're not going to have to polish up your bedpan."

"I thought that was a strange thing for you to say the other night. Now I understand."

"Understand? Just what is it you understand, Jack?"

"Fear can make a person do and say things they don't mean. I did that at the hospital last night. I sliced you up pretty good. It works like a safety net. In case you fall you're forewarned it's going to happen. You can say, I knew it would happen, or maybe…it's better this way. Anyway, it's all crap." He sat up and shoved himself against the headboard. "You don't really believe in free rides. Nor do you want it that way."

Sunni bit down on the inside of her cheek and tightened the sash around her waist with such force she nearly cut herself in two. In the beginning her plan had been just a few nights in his arms. After last night, she'd begun to think there might be a chance for more. This morning that chance had been shredded. No, torched, and what was left was a pile of ashes.

"This mess doesn't have a solution like one of your cases, Jack. I know you're the whatever-it-takes cop. The down-and-dirty-is-familiar-territory guy, but I don't need you to pick up with me where you left off with your father. Thanks, but no thanks."

His jaw jerked, and he lifted an eyebrow. A second later, he raised one naked knee and rested his arm there, displaying himself openly. Finally, he said, "Afraid to lean on someone, Sis? It's more than obvious you're hungry for a man in your bed. Afraid the guy can't stick it out for more than a week or two?"

Sunni swore, then went looking for her slippers.

All right, it was an excuse to keep from drooling over his marvelous package, or saying the wrong thing. She was furious with him, but, naked, Jack could make a million as a male centerfold—everything about him was larger than life.

Damn him for that. And damn him for being able to read her mind.

"Since you've been shooting insulin, can't get anyone to carry the ball? Is that it? How many guys have come and gone? We both know there hasn't been anyone recent because of the way you—"

"Shut up, Jack." Sunni was practically standing on her head, looking under the bed for her slippers when she found one. She reached, gripped the hard sole, then stood slowly.

"I used to brush Dad's teeth, too. Cream his feet to keep 'em soft. Didn't bother me, though."

"Go to hell, Jack. Better yet, go back to New Orleans." With that, Sunni hurled the slipper through the air. It made a loud smack as it hit him square between his eyes.

He grunted. Swore, then dropped his knee. The bedsprings groaned. Sunni didn't stick around after that; she raced through the door.

"Going for higher ground, Sis?"

"The kitchen," she hollered over her shoulder. "I need to eat breakfast in twenty minutes. You know us diabetics, Jack, we're a royal pain in the ass."

Sunni watched from the kitchen window as Jack leaned over and rested his forearm on a gray sedan, talking to the two detectives who had stood watch throughout the night.

Tom Mallory's home was in a quiet neighborhood.

The front yard was well taken care of with sturdy oak and elm trees to shelter the small two-story from the street. But Sunni wasn't interested in oaks and elms or how quiet the neighborhood was. What was distracting her from keeping breakfast on time was the nicest, tightest male butt in the city aimed straight at the kitchen window.

He shoved away from the car and turned around. The morning was cool and he'd pulled on his leather jacket before he'd gone outside. She could see his breath as he started back to the house. His stride was long and his dark hair moved freely in the wind.

The tough-guy jacket and faded jeans fit him, she decided. And the tough-guy city where he'd grown up fit him, too. He had never really told her why he'd relocated to New Orleans, but last night when he'd mentioned Tom Mallory, she had put two and two together. The death of his ex-partner had driven him away from his home and the job that fit him better than his made-to-order shirts and hip-hugging sexy jeans.

The door opened. She turned, her chin as high as she could get it without staring at the ceiling. He leaned against the door frame, his hands finding his jeans' front pockets, parting his jacket to show off his hell-raiser hard body. "I don't smell any breakfast, Sis. How come? Stove not working?" He looked at the clock on the wall next to the table. "You got eight minutes if you want to keep on your breakfast schedule."

Sunni glared at him, not liking him telling her what she already knew. "We're having cereal. It won't take me eight minutes to put a box on the table. More like thirty seconds." That's not what she had planned, but it was his fault she'd been unable to yank herself away from the window.

He didn't say anything to that, just kept staring—staring at the twins. For heaven's sake, now he had her calling them by that ridiculous name. Disgusted with herself, she stormed to the fridge and jerked it open, then bent over. "Mac? When are you going to pick him up?"

"He has to be awake before they'll release him. I'll pick him up around five. You miss him?"

"About as much as I'm going to miss you when you're out of my hair and back in New Orleans," she lied. "Eek!"

The sudden pinch on her butt cheek sent Sunni into orbit. On her way back down, he grabbed the milk carton out of her hand. "That's for this lump." He pointed to his forehead and the raised red welt, then walked to the table and set the milk down. When he turned around to face her, he was, again, ogling her.

"Knock it off, Jack." She spun around to retrieve the box of cereal she'd seen earlier in the cupboard.

Suddenly an arm came around her and hauled her back against steel muscles covered in soft leather and rugged denim. He bent his head and, next to her ear, whispered, "I'm the one who can carry the ball."

He kissed her ear, straightened quickly, then spun her and lifted her off her feet. A moment later she was sitting on the counter in pretty much the same vulnerable position he'd put her in last night. His hands clamped down on her knees and he jerked them wide and stepped forward. "Let's get something straight here. Whether you believe it or not, I'm *the man.* It's ironic, but your father told me that the day I left. He said, 'Whether I like it or not, Ward, you're the man.' He said it just like that. I didn't know how right he was then. But I do now."

"Jack...don't say that. Don't say anything."

"It's too late. If I think it, I say it, remember? So here goes. I love you. I love your husky voice, the way you smell. I love your sexy clothes. The way you chew your food." He grinned. "The way you moan when I'm inside you. I just can't think of anything that I don't love about you except your china cups." His hands slid up her thighs. "I mean it. I'm the man who can carry the ball, Sis."

He loved her. Sunni silently recited the words. It was a dream come true, to be loved by Jack Ward. But he was wrong. He might be the man for her, but she wasn't the woman for him. He deserved better. A woman who wouldn't be a noose around his neck. A healthy woman who wouldn't send him running to the hospital every other week if she got off her schedule and ate dinner an hour late.

"I know you're afraid I'm going to run, but I won't."

Everything that Jack was, and stood for, was in-your-face, I'm-ready-for-whatever. And, yes, that was the problem. If he said he loved her, he did. If he said he wouldn't run, he wouldn't, no matter what happened or how much he regretted making that kind of a commitment.

I lived at the hospital and I hated it. I brushed his teeth. Wiped his nose, the other end, too.

Sunni buried her misery with a false smile. "It's true I enjoy you in my bed, Jack. A good man, as they say, is hard to find. But sharing top-notch sex and a kitchen during a crisis situation is all we've been sharing. I don't feel the same way you feel. I'm sorry, but I don't think I ever will."

He stared at her for a long minute. Then, he asked, "You're sure?"

Forcing the lie between her teeth, Sunni nodded. "Sorry, Jack."

He glanced down at his watch. "Three minutes. Let's get you fed so you can keep on your schedule."

Chapter 13

Jackson was on the freeway with Mac laying beside him half-asleep—still groggy from his surgery—when something Lucky said the night before hit him. And as if his words had the power of the double-barreled *lupara* in the broom closet, they blew a hole in the case.

He and Lucky had been talking about rumors and bad guys. Lucky had mentioned cops being saints. The words weren't much by themselves, but Joe had used the words *saintly bastard* at the Shedd when they'd been talking about his mystery woman.

Hank had said there'd been talk Tom was on the take. He'd asked him to let him know first if he learned anything about Tom while he was in town.

As he headed back to Sunni, Jackson played the what-if game, then mentally made a list. After that, he concentrated on opportunity, human nature, and the odds. He thought about heartless bad boys and saintly cops, and decided his hunch was worth checking out.

He made a phone call to Hank, and after a few pointed questions, the odds climbed higher. And that's when he turned right on Ogden and punched in Joe's private number. "This is me," he said when he heard his friend's voice. "One question, bro."

"Okay, shoot."

"Was it Rhea?"

There was a long silence before the answer came. Then one word. "Yes."

The odds suddenly tipped the scale. "I'm on Ogden headed north. Meet me at her place. *Capiche?*"

"I have a key. We won't have to break in."

"And I thought Lucky was the one who lived dangerously. See you in twenty minutes."

Joe was already in front of Rhea Williams's house on Bliss Avenue when Jackson pulled up. As he climbed out of the rental car, leaving Mac asleep in the front seat, he studied his friend. Joe was leaning against his black Jag. He had traded his suit and tie in for a pair of jeans and a black leather jacket. He looked as tough as Lucky, puffing away on a cigarette with his dark sunglasses hiding his eyes.

Jackson quickly closed the distance. "Let's talk inside."

Without a word, Joe shoved away from the Jag and produced a key from his pocket. Inside the small house, Jackson followed him through the kitchen and into a feminine living room in pastel colors. Before Joey sat down on the gray sofa, he removed his sunglasses and laid them on the wooden coffee table.

Jackson took a seat on the piano bench not far away. "Okay, let's hear it."

Joey closed his eyes for a moment as if he needed to arrange the order of what he was going to say. When he opened them, he said, "I met her at the hospital. Lucky was getting stitched up. She was there getting a few of her own. Seems she ran into a door." He swore, his gaze unwavering as he stared Jackson down. "She was pretty bad off that time. Me and Lucky volunteered to take her home."

Jackson frowned. "Just like that?"

"Stud had been working for Frank for about a year at the time. Seemed appropriate."

"So Stud Williams is on the take. I never would have guessed that."

"Why not? Too saintly?"

There was that word again. Jackson shrugged. "I knew he was hard on Rhea."

"Hard on her? He beat her, Jacky. Beat her hard."

"I knew he was obsessed with her. Took after a couple of guys at the precinct once. They had made remarks about her long legs, and her being a natural blonde. When she divorced him, he damn near went crazy. She asked me and Tom to help her get this place. I moved her in here."

"She told me."

"Tom liked her a lot. He came to see her after the divorce. After his death, Stud became my partner, remember? It didn't last long. He liked things black-and-white and I'm color-blind so... Anyway, that's about the time I made the move to New Orleans. I called Hank on the way over here. He told me Rhea moved away about a week after I left town."

Joey said, "Stud stalked her. He wanted people to think that he had accepted the divorce but he never did."

"So you offered her a ride home that night. And then?"

"Nothing. Until it happened again. She was at the hospital when she called. He'd hurt her real bad that time. I went and got her."

"And then?"

Joey's jaw jerked. "I spent the night. Right here on this sofa. She was scared. Scared of the dark. Scared of the slightest noise. Hell, even of her own shadow."

"But not you." It wasn't a question.

"There was something going on between us from the moment we laid eyes on each other. I know that now. I can't explain it."

Jackson understood. It had been the same for him and Sunni. Smiling, he said, "You always did have a weakness for natural blondes."

"I never saw her bruise-free." Joey swore. "Stud hurt her in ways that I can't begin to describe, Jacky. I should have killed him. I regret that I didn't, but he was on Frank's payroll. And you know the rules I have to play by. I couldn't do it without bringing a bunch of hell down on all of us, so I didn't do anything." Joey closed his eyes and rested his head against the back of the couch. After a long minute, he opened them again. "Anyway, I was engaged to Sophia. I had no business looking at Rhea Williams. Sophia and I were suppose to be married before the end of the year."

"Did Stud know about you and Rhea?"

"No. And neither did Sophia. We were careful. Lucky was my watchdog."

"For how long?"

"Two months." Joey puffed on his cigarette. "Then one day I came here and she was gone. I tore the city apart looking for her. At first I thought Stud had done something to her. But he was looking for her, too. He even asked Frank to call in a few favors to help him find her. Frank put out feelers coast-to-coast. But it's like she just vanished. After that, Stud picked up the lease on this place. He told Frank he wanted to keep it in case Rhea came back."

"D'Lano?"

Joey stared at Jackson. "You think Sophia found out I was seeing Rhea behind her back and had her father kill her?"

"Grace Tandi disappeared and was never found. If Vito sent his wife to the bottom of Lake Michigan for adultery and got away with it, then a jealous fiancée with a father who's part of the organization and owns the biggest salvage yard in the city, could certainly make someone an ink spot under two tons of iron."

"Jeez, Jacky." Joey jerked to his feet. "I can't think that happened."

Jackson could see he had upset Joe more than he'd meant to, but facts were facts. "So Stud's been keeping this place just waiting for his ex-wife to come home. Somehow that doesn't fit."

"So she's dead?"

"Maybe, bro." He glanced around, saw a woman's pair of strapped white sandals tucked half under the couch. Frowning, he asked, "You know if those are Rhea's shoes?"

Joey glanced at the shoes Jackson had pointed to. "They look like hers."

Thinking that was just as strange as Stud paying on a second house when he already owned one on Ashland, Jackson got to his feet and walked down the hall to the bedroom. Peeking his head inside, he said, "Joe..."

As he stepped into what obviously had been Rhea Williams's bedroom, Joe appeared in the doorway. "What the hell is this?"

"It looks like someone's living here."

"And wearing Rhea's clothes?"

"So they're hers?"

"Yes."

Jackson studied the clothes laid out on the bed. Then turned to assess the underwear displayed on the dresser. "Not wearing," he said, "just looking."

"What?"

"A man obsessed with his ex-wife would want to stay close to her things. If you can't have the real thing, you settle. Substitute. Right?"

Joey released a string of obscenities.

"Let's have a look around. You take the other bedroom, I'll take the bathroom."

When they met back in the living room, Jackson said, "When we came through the kitchen I thought I saw a door. Closet?"

"Basement."

Jackson moved back into the kitchen and opened the door to the basement. Joe came up behind him and flipped on a light switch in the kitchen that lit up the stairwell and beyond. Following Jackson down the narrow stairs, he said, "There isn't much down here. Just storage for—"

There were no words to describe the sight that confronted them as Jackson and Joey came off the last step. Both men simply stared for several minutes.

Finally, Joey shouldered his way past Jackson to stare at the four walls that outlined the basement. Walls that were peppered with pictures and newspaper clippings.

Jackson gazed at the collection of memorabilia—traits of a psychotic madman. "Look." He pointed to a number of pictures of Rhea Williams with Tom Mallory. There were a half-dozen of the two of them. The two of them out to dinner, leaving the movie theater. Tom bringing her home. Tom leaving the house. The picture that got Jackson's attention was of Rhea crying at Tom's funeral. The picture had been placed in an square box outlined in black ink, with the words Justice Served written along the top.

He stared at the picture for a long time, knew what it meant. Finally he said, "Stud killed Tom."

"It looks that way, bro."

Jackson's heart started to hammer inside his chest. He scanned the next wall, this one dedicated entirely to Rhea Williams and her life with Stud—shared birthdays, a boat ride on the river, picnics in the backyard. But in all the pictures Rhea Williams was never smiling.

The next wall was devoted to Milo Tandi, Elizabeth Carpenter and Sunni. Clearly telling Jackson that—though he didn't understand Stud's motivation—he was certain he had killed Milo, as well as Elizabeth Carpenter.

There were no pictures of Rhea with Milo as there had been with Tom. Instead there were newspaper clippings of Milo's death. Sunni leaving Masado Towers, getting into a cab. Milo with Elizabeth Carpenter entering the Crown Plaza. Nothing, however, was old. All the pictures and newspaper articles were fairly recent—a month old at the most.

The next wall took Jackson by surprise. It was devoted to him. He didn't hear Joey come up behind him until his friend swore viciously. The next thing out of his mouth was "You're next, *mio fratello.* The son of a bitch wants you dead next."

Then to prove it was true, Joey pointed to an empty square box outlined in black ink with the words Justice Served above it.

He loved her. Sunni had replayed the words over and over again in her mind all afternoon. With Jackson gone to pick up Mac, it was the perfect chance to get a grip and fortify the lie she'd told him that morning. But every time she started to think about pushing Jack further away, his heavy voice claiming that he loved her drowned out everything else.

She knew the lie she'd told was for his own good. She couldn't...no, *wouldn't,* saddle him with a woman who someday might need him to brush her teeth.

When the knock came to the back door, she stood and peeked out the side window. Detective Williams had called an hour ago and she'd told him that Jackson wouldn't be back until after six. Seeing him now surprised her, but she swung the door open, anyway, and took a step back to let him enter the small kitchen. "Jack's not here," she offered.

"I know. I figured he wouldn't be back yet, but I thought I'd drop off the report on Libby… Ah, Elizabeth Carpenter. I've got a busy night planned, and…" He glanced around. "You alone?"

"Yes."

"Good idea, Jackson sneaking you out of the hospital like that." He glanced at the coffeepot. "Coffee sure smells good. Can you spare a quick cup?"

Sunni glanced at the folder. She was curious about the report. "Sure. Sit down."

He pulled a chair out at the table. Sunni noticed him wince as his left arm bumped the table. Like always, he was dressed in a sports jacket over a white shirt and tie. But today he was wearing jeans instead of dress slacks, and boots instead of loafers. He really did fit the typical detective, she thought, glancing at the notepad that stuck out of his jacket pocket as she brought him his coffee. "Sugar or cream?"

"Sugar, please."

"So—" Sunni placed a number of sugar packets on the table with a spoon, then sat "—can you tell me anything about Elizabeth?"

"I suppose it wouldn't hurt now that I'm convinced the case has taken a turn and you're no longer a suspect." He smiled, took a sip of the coffee. "She was definitely murdered. Jackson was right. Libby… Elizabeth Carpenter had drugs in her system, but that's not what killed her. She drowned."

Sunni couldn't imagine a more horrible death. "Poor Elizabeth."

Detective Williams added a bit more sugar to his coffee, stirred. ''She was already out of it before she died. She didn't feel anything.''

''How can you be sure? Is that what the report says?''

''Not exactly. But she'd snorted a lot of white lightning that night. She passed out before she went swimming. I guarantee it.''

''If she drowned, how can you tell it was murder?''

''It's murder when someone deliberately feeds an addict too much candy for the sole purpose of killing them once they've passed out.''

Sunni stood and walked to the sink to get a drink of water. ''But you can't know that's what happened without...'' As she ran water in the glass, she glanced out the window and realized that the detectives in the unmarked cruiser were no longer out front. She was about to mention it when she heard the scraping of the detective's chair on the tile floor. She turned and found Stud standing in the middle of the room pointing a gun at her.

''I know that's what happened, Miss Blais, because I was the one who fed her the white lightning.'' He grinned, seemingly pleased with the effect his confession had on her.

Sunni gripped the counter to stay on her feet, unable to believe what she was hearing. ''You? You killed Elizabeth?''

''You don't look like you'd be very strong.'' He rubbed his shoulder. '''Course, the paperweight was crystal, wasn't it?''

''Oh, God!''

He shook his head. ''God isn't going to be able to

help you, Miss Blais. And neither will Jackson or that hairy partner of his. No, it looks like I'm the only one on the job today.''

His gaze traveled to the window. ''The boys were anxious to take a break. They went for some coffee and smokes. I told them not to rush back, that I'd watch over you until they got back. Only we're not going to be here when they get back.''

''I don't understand. You're Jackson's friend. Why are you doing this?''

''Friend…ex-partner.'' He shrugged. ''They're a dime a dozen to Jackson. He's had more partners than any cop alive.''

''I still don't understand.''

''This has nothing to do with wanting to hurt you, Miss Blais. I've been seeking justice for an old unsolved crime for three years. A month ago I uncovered evidence that reopened the case. I always believed that there were two men involved in the deception. I just couldn't prove it. Milo and Libby, and yes, you, were all invaluable in bringing this case to a close. I learned you were Clide Blais's daughter by accident, but what a gem that piece of information was. It was so easy after that. Libby stealing your scarves. Killing Milo at the Crown Plaza and making it look like you'd done it. Without you becoming a suspect, Jackson wouldn't have been sent back to Chicago. 'Course, I made sure he'd come. But you really were the key.''

''What does Jackson have to do with this?''

''He's the second man, Miss Blais. A criminal.''

''You're mistaken. Jack would never—''

''Shut up! It was an ingenious plan setting you up

so he'd come back. I executed everything perfectly. Every detail was cross-examined again and again. A good detective pays attention to details.''

Sunni glanced at the clock. Jack wouldn't be back for at least a half hour. He wasn't going to be able to save her—Detective Williams was right about that. ''Why Elizabeth?''

''The lovely Libby was the perfect accomplice. She was very loyal to her habit, and to me since I was the one feeding it. But weaknesses can be a deadly business, as I'm sure you know, Miss Blais. Last night yours nearly cost you your life. I look at it as having done Libby a favor, really. She was supporting a demanding habit…a weakness. One that would have eventually killed her…same as you. This way she went quietly and quite peacefully. And since I have no malice toward you, your death will be just as painless. You'll just slip away.''

He was going to kill her. Sunni responded without thinking. ''You're a monster,'' Sunni screamed, then sent the half-full glass of water flying through the air.

The shot that rang out seconds later shattered the window above the sink. Still screaming, Sunni tried to reach the door but he caught her around the waist and dragged her to the floor. She went down kicking and swinging her arms, but she was no match for a madman who had been a cop for ten years.

Stud's fist punch sent Sunni clutching her stomach and gasping for air. The second rendered her unconscious.

While Jackson stood staring at the proof he needed to put Stud Williams in a cold, dark cell, his phone rang. He pulled the phone from his jacket pocket and flipped it open. "Ward here."

"Detective Ward?"

"That's me, who's this?"

"Fletcher. You know. Me and Guthrie are staking out the Mallory house. Only Miss Blais must have left the house, sir. She must've taken a ride somewhere."

"A ride?"

"Yeah, with Detective Williams. He's not here, either, like he said he'd be."

Jackson felt dizzy, as if his lungs had collapsed and no air was reaching his brain. Or maybe he'd just been knifed in the back. Either way, he couldn't breathe, could barely think. He heard himself say, "He took her…but you don't know where or when?"

"We went for coffee, sir. Detective Williams suggested it. He said he'd watch her until we got back. But when we got back—"

"Keep trying his cell phone. I'll give you the number." As he recited the digits, Jackson turned to look at Joe, who was back staring at the many pictures of Rhea Williams. "Let me know if you raise him."

He disconnected, then phoned Sunni at the house just to make sure Fletcher was on the level. When she didn't answer, he called her apartment. When the answering machine clicked on, he swore, jammed the phone into his pocket and said, "Stud just made his move. He's got Sunni. Let's go."

They took separate cars. Both men, breaking all the speed limits, arrived back at Tom Mallory's house twenty minutes later. As they pulled up Fletcher and Guthrie were in the front yard arguing.

Jackson jumped from the car. "Know anything more?" he hollered on his way to the house. When the two men continued to argue, he stopped, pulled his .38 out from inside his jacket and fired it into the air. When the shot rang out, both detectives hit the ground and went fumbling for their weapons. "I asked a question, you sons of bitches! Any news?"

"No…sir." Fletcher scrambled to his feet. Guthrie stayed down. "Oh, except the kitchen window's broken. Looks like a gunshot caused it. No blood inside, though."

After a quick check of the house, Jackson picked up the file that lay on the table and opened it. Along with the report on Elizabeth Carpenter was a short message from Stud. *Meet me at Rhea's. You know the place.*

As he was exiting the house, Fletcher was helping his aging partner to his feet and dusting him off. When Jackson strode past them, he offered a quick punch to Guthrie that put him back on his ass, and when Fletcher looked up in surprise, he got an elbow up his nose that nearly tore him a new nasal passage.

While they moaned and rolled around in the front yard, both nursing broken noses, Jackson joined Joey in the street. "He wants me to meet him at Rhea's place," he said, handing over the note.

Joey leaned against his Jag and studied the message. Finally he said, "He doesn't know we've been there. That could be an advantage. We know what he's been up to. We know he killed Tom, and why. But it's unclear why he wants you dead." He rubbed his jaw. "He doesn't mention Sunni—what do you make of that?"

"I don't know." Jackson's chest ached, as if someone had ripped out his heart. It was how he'd felt last night when he'd found Sunni in the storage room at Silks.

Why hadn't he taken her with him today? Why had he let her out of his sight?

"He wants you, not her. He's using her as bait. That's all she is. Right?"

"He killed Milo and Elizabeth Carpenter, and they were bait."

"We don't know that for sure."

"I know it!" Jackson lost it. "I know it, Joe!"

Joey reached out and grabbed Jackson around the neck. Nose to nose, he said, "He wants something else from you, do you hear? He could have flown to New Orleans, popped you and flew back out. He wants something more and he's not going to kill Sunni before he gets it. *Capiche?*"

When Joey released him, Jackson checked his watch. "It's almost seven. Sunni's diabetes makes this a race against time. She's off her schedule already."

"Her schedule?"

"Food, Joe. If Sunni doesn't eat regularly, she'll have another insulin reaction like she had last night." Jackson's cell phone rang. Keeping his voice steady, he said, "Yeah."

"You haven't e-mailed me today. What the hell's going on, Ward? You forget why I sent you back home? You're not on vacation, you know."

The last thing he needed was Clide grilling him right now. "I've been busy." Jackson peeked into his car window. Mac was still lethargic, still sleeping off the anesthetic from his surgery. ''I can't talk right now, Chief.''

''How's Sunni?''

He glanced at Joe who was pulling his own phone from his pocket. ''She's holding on.''

''Finally got sprung from the hospital. You need me to jump on a plane? You think it would help if I showed up at the CPD and threw my weight around? Speed things up?''

''No. Stay put. Gotta go.''

He disconnected before Clide could mention Sunni again, his ear turned to the last of Joe's conversation.

''Get yourself over to Bliss Avenue and stake out 623. I want to know who goes in and comes out. The minute you know anything, call me back. And get in touch with Lucky and find out where the hell he is. We could use him about now. ''

''That house is too damn small to get inside without being heard,'' Jackson offered the minute Joey hung up. ''And Mac's still doped up, he's not going to be worth a damn.''

''Gates said give him ten minutes. He's not far from Bliss Avenue.'' Joey opened the car door and tossed the phone onto the leather seat, then popped opened the glove compartment. He reached inside and pulled out a sleek black 9 mm Beretta and slid it into his pocket. ''I don't have four legs, and as many teeth, but I'm willing to back you.'' He patted his jacket pocket. ''Whatever you need, *mio fratello*. I'm here for you.''

Twelve minutes later Joey's cell phone rang. He reached into his car to retrieve it off the seat. ''What do you see, Gates?''

"I got Detective Williams pulling into the garage at 623."

"He alone?"

"No."

"Can you see who's with him?"

"Police Chief Mallory."

"You sure?"

"I'm sure."

"No one else?"

"No one."

Jackson waited until the phone landed in the leather bucket seat, then asked, "Is she with him?"

"No. He's at the house. But Sunni's not with him. Hank Mallory is. What do you make of that?"

No Sunni… Jackson turned away, felt his world tilt.

"That doesn't mean she's dead, Jacky. He could have stashed her somewhere."

"Like he did Elizabeth Carpenter?" Jackson squeezed his eyes shut. It was like a damn nightmare. A nightmare that he wasn't going to wake up from.

"The only way we're going to know what the son of a bitch did with her is to go and confront him," Joey said. "So let's do it."

Jackson started back to the house. Over his shoulder he yelled, "I've got to get a couple of things. You take off. I'll be right behind you."

Sunni was bound and gagged, and she was cold. Shivering, she stared into the darkness and wondered where she was.

She was lying on her back in a small black box of some kind. Her hands were tied in front of her and so were her ankles.

She was bruised and sore from being used as a punching bag for Stud Williams's fist, but she was alive. But for how long?

Her confrontation with Williams in Tom Mallory's kitchen had completely thrown her. One minute he was a police detective doing his job, and the next minute he was aiming a gun at her, his eye glazed over like a madman's.

When she'd tossed the water at him, she had only one objective—to get away. But she'd realized her mistake the minute she'd seen him double up his fist. She had tried to protect herself, but he was bigger and so much stronger. And his fists had been so angry, and so determined.

He'd split her lip and she could still taste the blood. Her stomach ached and her jaw throbbed. Her bruises wouldn't kill her, but the cold and her reaction to it would. It would steadily seep into her bones and numb her senses, and eventually her body would succumb to its own inherent weakness—her diabetes.

Your death with be painless. You'll just slip away.

She didn't want to die, but her fear was for more than just herself. Stud Williams was an evil man and he wasn't done killing. She could see it in his eyes, see it in the way he spoke Jack's name. Jack was in terrible danger.

Stud Williams had ripped her blouse off and taken her shoes. She didn't understand why that was, why he'd left her in just jeans and her bra. But the cold night air was definitely advancing her condition more rapidly—the black box felt like a freezer.

The cold made her sleepy and she knew if she

closed her eyes she would just slip away as Williams said.

She'd begun to feel nauseous and a little confused—the warning signs were closing in on her like a well-planned ambush. She needed to fight the weakness, fight the urge to close her eyes.

She concentrated on Jack, pictured him in her mind—pictured his warm hands on her body and his hot breath on her neck, on her breasts. She imagined him inside her, hard and pulsing, setting her on fire—an internal fire that warmed her from the top of her head to the tips of her very cold toes.

No, she wouldn't surrender and let the cold take her. If she kept her eyes open and her thoughts on Jack loving her and stroking her with his warm hands and kissing her with his hot mouth, she would survive.

Chapter 14

Jackson entered Rhea Williams's kitchen with his .38 in one hand and Lucky's *lupara* in the other. The house was dark, except for a dim light coming from the basement. As he neared the open door, he heard Stud say, ''Come on down, partner. Join the party.''

Before descending the stairs, he handed Joe the shotgun, then motioned for him to remain in the kitchen. Their plan was lean and straightforward. But with so little time, and only one way into the basement, the odds were definitely in Stud Williams's favor.

Jackson descended the stairs. On reaching the bottom step, he saw Hank Mallory on the floor in a corner. He'd been shot—a shoulder wound that was bleeding heavy but wouldn't kill him.

His eyes locked with Jackson's in a silent plea to avenge Tom, but that would have to wait. It was Sunni who concerned him at the moment, and he prayed Joe was right. He prayed that Stud felt he still needed her, and she was alive.

He eased off the last step and focused on Stud where he sat behind a small metal work desk with a .38 in his hand. He sat close to the wall, which protected his back and, at the same time, offered him a perfect view of Rhea's pictures and the madness that surrounded her.

"So what do you think? Did you ever imagine that your old partner was capable of such an outstanding job of detective work?"

Playing dumb, Jackson glanced around as if it was the first time he'd seen the walls. "What's all this about, Stud?"

"It's about justice, Jackson. A man's wife is his most prized possession. Three years ago Rhea was taken from me. It was a crime against me and God. Tommy boy was a fool flaunting his lust for my wife, and he paid for it quick and easy. But you...you were more clever. The evidence wasn't there, not until a month ago, that is." He shrugged. "'Course, justice always prevails, isn't that right...partner?"

Jackson glanced at Tom's funeral picture. "So you killed Tom because he was seeing Rhea?"

"He slept with my wife. He made the choice to live or die."

"She divorced you, Stud."

"That was a mistake. A mistake we were working out. But then you came along and confused her."

"You're wrong, Stud. You're wrong about all of this."

"No. I have proof." Stud gestured to the silver chain and cross on the desk. "I found that behind Rhea's dresser a month ago. I knew there was someone else lusting after my wife, someone besides Tommy boy. When I'd come to see her, I could smell cigarette smoke. Tommy-boy didn't smoke. Rhea didn't, either. I knew you were a smoker. I guess I just never thought you were her type.

"I wanted to kill you quick when I first found the evidence. I'd been trying to find out who the second man was for years. The man responsible for taking my wife away from me. Then I realized that 'quick' wasn't the answer. I wanted to show you what a good piece of detective work I'd done. You know how hard it is to stick with a tough case, Jackson. Especially when you keep hitting dead ends."

"Stud, you're wrong."

He pointed to the cross. "That's your chain. I remember seeing it around your neck. You convinced Rhea to leave me and go to New Orleans, didn't you? And what happened after that? Did you throw her away after you were finished with her?"

"You're crazy, Stud. Rhea never came to New Orleans."

"A crime was committed here and I'm honor-bound to extract justice. Now, ease that Diamondback of yours to the floor, *partner,* then shove it away. Go on, or I'll kill Mallory."

Jackson did as he was told. He squatted and sent the gun across the room. It split the distance between him and Stud—some twenty feet. As he eased back up, he said, "Where's Sunni?"

"Miss Blais is somewhere cold and dark, and all alone." Stud patted a shoe box on the table. "But there's still time. She could be rescued. Only I won't save her unless you tell me where Rhea is. Where has my wife been living for three years?"

Someplace cold and dark, and all alone. Jackson couldn't help but think about Elizabeth Carpenter and how she'd been found in a cold, dark place. He stared at the box and prayed that Sunni was still alive. Prayed for a miracle.

"Does Clide Blais know you've been sleeping on the job, Jackson? Sleeping with his daughter?" He grinned. "That's right. I broke into your apartment at the Wilchard and watched from across the alley. She really is a lovely woman. And generous, too."

Jackson felt another knife twist into his gut. "You're a dead man, Stud."

He shook his head, his grin gone. "No, *you're* dead, and Miss Blais will be, too, if you don't tell me where Rhea's hiding. Where's my wife living, Jackson?"

"I don't..." Jackson paused. "First I see Sunni and make sure she's alive. Then we'll deal."

"Cops don't deal with criminals, Jackson, you know that. Especially when I'm the one holding all the cards."

Suddenly Stud shoved back his chair and aimed his .38 at Hank Mallory's head where he sat on the floor. "You got two seconds to tell me where Rhea is or this good old boy is dead. Stall much longer and Miss Blais will be, too. I figure she's got maybe an hour left at the most."

The stairs creaked a warning just before Joey appeared on the stairway with the *lupara* slung on his shoulder.

"Masado? What are you doing here?"

"I came to help out."

"I don't need your help, or Frank's. This is my business. And I'll take care of it my own way."

"You have it wrong, Stud. Everything wrong, as a

matter a fact.'' Joey's eyes shifted to the cross on the desk. ''When Rhea was afraid she liked wearing that. She said it made her feel safer. I hadn't taken it off in—'' he glanced at Jackson ''—when was it, Jacky? When did Vina give us those crosses? Were we sixteen, or was it fifteen?''

There was a moment of silence, then the shock and outrage of what Joey had just confessed sent the situation over the edge. Stud had been aiming his .38 at Hank Mallory; now he jerked sideways and started to bring his arm toward the stairway. ''You? It was you? You bastard!''

A fact that had always been understated on the streets of Chicago was Joey Masado's expertise with a knife. As fast as Jackson was with a gun, and Lucky with his fists, Joe was equally as fast with a knife. Just before he hurled the expensive steel at his hip, he said, ''I should have killed you three years ago, you son of a bitch.'' Then the knife was whistling through the air and into Stud's gun arm above the elbow.

Stud cried out and struggled to recover. In those brief seconds Joe sailed over the stair railing, at the same time Jackson dove for his .38. Seconds later, Stud fired on everything in the room that was moving. The gunfire was rapid, backed by rage and desperation. While he and Joey were rolling around, dodging the rain of bullets, Jackson yelled, ''Don't kill him, Joe! We need him to find Sunni!''

Six shots later—Stud's .38 empty—Jackson rolled to his feet and sprang over the metal desk. Plowing into Stud, he knocked him flat on his back. ''Where is she?'' he snarled, gripping Stud's shirt and driving his iron fist into his jaw. Blinded by his own rage and fear, he swung his fist again and again. ''Where is she?''

Spitting blood, Stud said, ''Kill me, then. Go on, Jackson.''

''You're not going to die,'' Jackson snarled. ''That would be too easy. You're not getting off easy, Stud. Not one minute for the rest of your life!'' That said, he drove his fist forward in one last unforgiving punch that rendered the madman unconscious.

His chest heaving, Jackson shoved to his feet and ripped the top off the box on the desk. Inside was the pink silk blouse that Sunni had on earlier, along with her shoes. The blouse had been torn, and it was spattered with blood. The sight sickened him, and he squeezed his eyes shut for a moment as a dozen questions ran through his mind.

''I know what you're thinking,'' Joey said, moving past him to see to Hank Mallory, ''but he wouldn't have told you where she is, anyway.''

Jackson knew Joe was right. He turned and hunkered down by his ex-boss. ''Hank, did you see Sunni? Did Stud say anything about where he hid her?''

''Only that it was someplace where you wouldn't find her until it was too late.'' Hank groaned. ''He tricked me, Jackson. I fell for it, and I'm sorry. I just saw the pictures of Tom and went crazy.''

''What time did you meet him?''

After Hank explained how Stud had called him, and what time that was, he said, ''He picked me up at police headquarters. He told me he'd found evidence that could shed some light on Tom's murder. I guess he knew just what to say to make me go with him.''

Jackson turned to Joe. ''The time frame is too tight

for Stud to have dropped Sunni off somewhere before he picked up Hank. She's still at Tom's house somewhere, or here.''

''Gates only saw two people in the car, Jacky.''

''I've been with Stud the entire time since he picked me up.'' Hank groaned again as Jackson and Joey helped him stand. ''Maybe the trunk of the car, but don't waste time searching anywhere else around here.''

Anxious at the possibility that Sunni could be close by, Jackson grabbed the silk blouse from the box and raced up the stairs. As he left the house he heard Mac barking. Relieved that the dog might be able to offer him some help, he jogged to the car and opened the door. When Mac jumped out, he let the dog sniff Sunni's blouse. ''Find her, boy. Find Sis.''

They searched Stud's car but they came up with nothing. When Joe showed up on the porch, Jackson said, ''We're headed back to Tom's house. Call me if you think of anything, or if Stud comes around and you can get him to talk. I'll call if I locate her.''

The closer they got to Tom Mallory's house, the more agitated Mac became. Hopeful, Jackson pulled up fast, leaned over and popped the passenger door to let Mac out. The dog bolted from the car and in a flash he was dropping his nose to the ground.

While Mac skirted the house, Jackson grabbed the flashlight from the glove compartment and followed him to a toolshed. The dog tore into the wooden door with no hesitation—sore mouth and a dozen-plus stitches didn't slow him down one bit.

Jackson pulled his .38, called Mac off, then shot the padlock off the door. Swinging it wide, Mac dove in first.

Along one wall was a built-in storage box with a hinged top. Mac was already attacking the box before Jackson reached it. Quickly, he tossed the lid up and sent the light beaming into the box.

The sight of Sunni bound and gagged inside twisted Jackson's gut. But there was no time for guilt, or emotion of any kind, as he saw her chest slowly moving up and down, only action.

"You'll be all right," he promised, then lifted her out of the box and gently laid her down. Working fast, every second critical, he pulled a narrow box from his shirt pocket with a syringe taped on top and went through the steps to prepare the emergency injection of glucagon he'd picked up last night before leaving the hospital. "This will fix you up, Sis," he guaranteed. "Then I'll get you in the house and warm you up."

She was semiconscious, her eyes open, and yet she wasn't with him. Jackson recognized the empty look. He'd seen it a hundred times in his father's eyes. Only today he wasn't thinking about how much he hated or feared that look, or how cheated he'd felt as a boy that Harold Ward had died too soon. No, today he was only grateful for the knowledge his father had given him, and the ability and experience to act on it in an emergency situation.

So on instinct, with steady hands—and Mac hovering close by—he pinched a thin layer of Sunni's abdomen and injected the hormone he knew would save her life.

Stud Williams was arrested and booked for the murder of Milo Tandi, Tom Mallory and Elizabeth

Carpenter the next morning. The buzz circulating at the CPD was loud, and the name most mentioned surrounding the buzz was Jackson Ward. The story claimed the loose cannon had single-handedly brought a killer to justice, and along with his K-9 super dog, had saved his police chief's daughter from certain death.

The rumors made no mention of the affiliation Stud Williams had with organized crime and the Masado family, or the fact that Hank Mallory had been escorted to the hospital by a man driving a black Jag.

No, the buzz had been all about the loose cannon, only he hadn't heard any of it. Last night, Jackson had taken a midnight flight back to New Orleans.

As the voice grew louder from inside Clide Blais's office, the tension mounted outside in the lobby. It was a sure bet Clide was chewing tail again, slicing off ears and taking the detective standing in front of his desk off at the knees, all at the same time gripping his antacid bottle and trying to get the cap off.

The heat inside the precinct was as insufferable as the heat outside. Today the news report was pridefully claiming the New Orleans high would reach ninety-five degrees, the humidity a suffocating eighty-nine percent.

Leaning against the lobby's front desk, Jackson watched his boss through his office window. He'd been back in town less than a day and it felt like he'd never left. His jeans were sticking to him, and his shirt clung to his chest like a wet wash rag. Last night, as he'd left O'Hare, Chicago had clear skies and was fifty-eight degrees.

Yeah, he'd gone and done it again. He'd pushed

too hard after Sunni had surfaced from her nightmare. He'd tossed it in her face how damn vulnerable she was, then how much she needed a man around to take care of her.

His mother had been right…again. Out of fear he'd stuck his foot in his mouth and hurt the woman he loved, instead of putting the blame squarely on his own shoulders where it belonged. The truth was, if he'd been doing his job, Sis would never have been placed in danger.

No wonder she'd kicked his ass out of the house and her life the minute she could stand on her own two feet. Which hadn't taken all that long. The glucagon had worked like a charm, as he knew it would.

When Clide glanced out his window, Jackson nodded. Two seconds later the young detective—minus his ears—was scrambling out of the chief's office muttering "good luck" as he hustled past the NOPD loose cannon.

Jackson mumbled, "In this business, junior, never rely on luck. What you need is iron balls, a steel head and earplugs. And don't let anyone tell you different."

"Ward, get in here! This ain't a social club."

Jackson set his jaw, sauntered into his chief's office and closed the door. Stopping at the window, he eyed the crew that had suddenly congregated to watch and listen. He waved, offered a smile—which was rarely seen inside the precinct—then pulled the shade closed.

"So tell me everything. Sunni called this morning. She told me at no time was she in any danger. But frankly, I got the feeling she was covering your ass. Why would she do that, Ward?"

"I don't know, Chief. She say anything else?"

"Not much." Clide lowered his voice, and Jackson got the feeling that he didn't want anyone out front to hear their conversation. "She told me she's a diabetic. Told me she'd been avoiding telling her mother and me for some time. She said you have experience with that sort of thing."

"My father was a diabetic," Jackson offered.

"So give me your honest opinion, Ward. Is my daughter too sick to be on her own? At the moment it don't sound like she's got a man in her life that'll take care of her."

Jackson thought through his answer. "Your daughter is a smart woman, Chief. She's aware of the health risks she faces, and she's on top of them."

"But?"

"But it would be better for her if she had someone to lean on."

"She must have friends, Ward."

"She does."

"But I'm right, ain't I? There's no man in her life?"

Jackson didn't hesitate with his answer, Clide was eyeing him too closely. "No, Chief, there's no man."

Clide leaned back in his chair and stroked the gray mustache skirting his upper lip. "Got a call from Hank Mallory. He wants you back in Chicago."

Jackson was surprised, but he was careful not to show it.

"He'd like you to head up his Special Investigation Unit. It would get you off the street some. And get you an office. Does the job appeal to you, Ward?"

It appealed to him, all right. There were a dozen reasons why, and only a couple of them had to do with the job. Only he wasn't going to mention any of them to Clide. Not right now, anyway. He said, "I think I can do that job."

"Hell, yes, you can do that job. There isn't any doubt in my mind that you're *the man.* The best damn man for..." Clide flushed. "Ah...I'm prepared to make good on my promise, Ward. If you want to pack your bags and head back to Chicago, then I'll get busy with the paperwork. I meant everything I said ten days ago. Rescue Sunni, and you can have whatever it is you want. Name it, and it's yours."

He came to the window late at night. He came to gaze across the alley. He came half-naked, wearing his jeans low on his marvelous hips and taunting her with the memories they had made in ten crazy, stressful, incredible days.

That's right, two days ago Jack had moved back to Chicago. Sunni still couldn't believe it. He'd moved back without telling her, and he'd moved back into the Wilchard.

She had called her father the minute she'd learned of it. And he'd gladly offered her the whole story. He told her that Jack had accepted a job from Hank Mallory, a promotion at the CPD.

She should be angry, and a small part of her was—he hadn't bothered to call her or even come by to see her since he'd gotten back. But there was more going on inside her head and her heart, so much more.

Today she'd gone to see Jack's mother, and after a long two-hour talk with Lavina Ward, she'd made a decision, a decision that had driven her into action minutes ago.

When the knock came, Sunni was waiting at the

front door. Dressed in a red silk robe and a skimpy bra and thong to match, she swung the door open with a fixed false look of surprise on her face. ''Oh, it's you.''

''Oh, it's you?'' He blew into the apartment with his shirttails flying, his jeans low on his hips, and no socks in his shoes. ''What the hell was that just now!''

He was talking about the fact that six minutes ago she'd flashed him—and old man Ferguson—from the terrace. She would never have done it at that precise moment if she'd known the ninety-year-old man had been stargazing out his window. But she hadn't seen him standing there until he'd waved. And, anyway, it was all Jack's fault. He'd driven her to desperate measures.

Sunni studied his rigid stance and heavy scowl. Studied all six feet three inches of his iron will and rock-solid strength. He was possibly the strongest, most durable man she had ever met. Certainly the most unforgettable—with just one kiss, Jack Ward had forever changed her life. ''What's that look for, Jack? Stub your toe on the way over here?''

''Do you want to explain what you were doing damn near giving Crammer Ferguson a heart attack?''

''He was smiling, Jack, not gasping and clutching his heart.'' On hearing Mac bark out on the terrace, Sunni headed for the slider. As he entered the living room wagging his tail, she bent down and kissed his head, then said, ''I bought some entertainment for you today, sweetheart. Three hours of Westminster. The complete, unedited version.''

While Mac curled up on the sofa, Sunni popped the tape in the video recorder and turned on the TV.

When she came back around, Jack was still scowling. She scowled back. "You've been living at the Wilchard for two days without saying a word, Jack. Why?"

"It's only temporary. Until me and Mac find something more permanent."

"That's not the point, Jack. You're back in Chicago. Why?"

"Hank offered me a position in special investigations. Promised me my own office."

"And that's important?"

He shrugged, his gaze settling on the twins. Yes, she'd finally accepted the name he'd given them and actually missed hearing him call her breasts by that silly name. Which meant she was utterly and helplessly in love with this man and was no longer willing to deny it.

She should have told him that, and more, the night he'd rescued her from the toolshed. It would have been the perfect time to let go of her fears and just curl up in his very capable arms and confess everything she was feeling. Only he'd started in on how vulnerable she was and she'd gotten so angry that she had continued on with the lie.

"You shouldn't be out on the terrace dressed like that. This city is full of—"

"Snakes," Sunni finished for him. "If you don't like the view maybe you should stay away from your window."

"I never said I didn't like it. What I don't like is you giving some old guy like Crammer a turn-on."

Her gaze traveled to Jack's crotch.

He swore. "All right, right now I'm as hard as a steel pipe. Torturing me like this—"

"Torturing you? And what have you been doing to me for the past two nights. Last night your jeans were unzipped and—" Sunni snapped her mouth shut.

"And what? Come on. Say it. Admit you were watching me."

"Okay, Jack, I was watching you."

He started toward her.

Sunni backed up in the direction of the hall. "I told you, Jack, I don't need a nursemaid. Or someone to brush my teeth."

He stopped. "When I told you I loved you I wasn't offering you pity, or maid service. I was offering hot sex every night. Egg soufflé and orange juice in the morning. And company in the shower."

"And is that offer still on the table, Jack?"

One dark brow hiked up. "What exactly are you asking, Sis?"

Sunni angled her head, took a minute to study his brilliant green eyes. He really didn't know, she decided. She'd told her lie too well. He had no idea how desperately she loved him. His mother was right.

"Jack, first you need to know that I've never seduced a man in my life, in or out of the shower. And then you need to know that I went to see your mother. I like her a lot. Thirdly, you need to know that I lied."

"Lied? Again…"

Sunni smiled. "I figured you'd say that."

"Well, if I think it, I—"

"Say it. Yes, I know."

"What did you lie about?"

"I was afraid, Jack. That's why I told the lie, but now—"

"Afraid of what, Sis?"

"Afraid that someday you'd regret loving me if I

told you how I really felt. I love you so much, and the thought of saddling you with a sick woman who would someday become a royal pain in your amazingly tight incredible ass… Well I—''

''Say that again?''

Hands on her hips, Sunni scowled at him. ''You know you have an incredible ass, Jack. I'm not going to stroke your ego about something we both know is fact.''

''Not that part. There was a real nice couple of words somewhere in the middle.''

Sunni smiled. ''Oh… The part where I said, I love you.''

''Yeah, that's it.''

''I do love you, Jack. I have for days. Actually, I think I fell in love with you the minute you vampired my lip.''

''So you've had me dangling on a hook for days. Is that what you're saying?''

He started to advance on her. ''Jack, don't be angry.'' Sunni scurried down the hall and into the bedroom. Backing up, she felt the bed behind her. ''You're upset. And I guess you have a right to be.''

He didn't stop until he was inches from her, and his chest was brushing against hers. ''As the old saying goes, Sis. With that little confession you're… screwed.''

''Oh… Then I'm in big trouble.''

''Yeah…you could say that.'' He leaned into her and brushed his lower body against her. ''It looks like you've made your bed…with me in it.'' That said, he tumbled her onto the bed and wedged his knee between her legs. Forcing them wide, he fit himself against her.

"Jack…"

"Before things get any hotter, you have to know something, Sis. I was coming back. Whether I got the job or not. I was coming back."

"Because you love me," she whispered.

"Yes. Because I love you. And because I'm the man."

Hours later Jackson stood on the terrace with Sunni wrapped in a blanket curled against him. The sky was clear and there was a slight breeze. Chicago was lit up all the way to Lake Shore Drive and beyond, and from the Crown Plaza the view was spectacular.

"Ask me again, Jack."

He gazed down at her, unable to believe that she was in his arms. "Ask you what?"

"You know, what you asked me when I was—"

"Soaring, or diving?"

"Moaning. I think I was moaning when you popped the question."

He angled his head and looked down at her. "A man's ego is a delicate thing. If the answer is no, I don't think—"

Sunni reached down and squeezed him through his jeans.

He jumped. "Be careful! Wreck me, and then where will you be?"

"Out shopping for Super Glue, I suppose? I'm certain that's a one-of-a-kind." She sobered. "Maybe you didn't really mean it."

"I mean everything I say, Sis. You should know that by now."

"Then ask me again."

"Okay." He turned her to face him. "Sis, will you marry me…and Mac?"

"Maybe you should read my medical file first and then—"

Jackson shook his head. "I don't need to read anything. Say yes, so we can start celebrating…again." He opened the blanket and gazed inside. "The twins look anxious."

She went up on tiptoes and kissed him. "Oh yes, Jack. Yes, I would love to marry you."

"Thank you, God," he sighed, then scooped her up into his arms and started back inside.

"I can't wait to call Mom and Dad in the morning."

Jackson headed for the shower. "Let's hold off on that for a few days, sweet thing. Just until we're sure your father's ulcer is really on the mend."

"He's going to be so surprised."

"He's going to be more than that, honey." He set her down in the bathroom and tugged the blanket off her.

"A midnight shower, Jack?"

He grinned. "About this shower, Sis. You never did say what that's all about. What's going on in there?"

She opened the etched-glass door and turned on the water. Beautifully naked, she glanced over her satin-smooth shoulder. "A tip for the future, Jack. If you ever have questions about what's going on in our shower, all you need to do is look up. Sometimes, a picture truly is worth a thousand words."

Epilogue

Two days later Jackson found himself in Joe's office staring out the window waiting on the rain and Lucky. He'd called an hour ago and had asked Jackson to meet him in Joe's office.

"So when's the wedding?" Joey asked.

"We haven't pinned down the date. We still haven't called Clide."

"Sweating what Daddy's going to say?"

Jackson rubbed his jaw. "You don't know the half of it."

Joey chuckled. "You're still one lucky bastard, Jacky. Sunni's a beautiful lady."

"That she is, Joe. I feel like the luckiest man in the world." He turned from the window, grinning. In fact, he'd been grinning nonstop since Sis had told him she loved him.

"Where's Mac this morning?"

"Downstairs with Sunni. He likes tagging along behind her these days. I think he's a little jealous."

When the phone rang, Joey picked it up. "Yeah? Okay. We're both here." When he disconnected, he said, "Lucky's on his way up. He sounded strange."

"Strange, how?"

"Sober" was Joey's answer. "I'll be glad to find out where the hell he's been. Gates didn't even have a number where he could be reached. Frank's been all over me for days for letting him run off without knowing where or why. Hell, it's been six days."

When the door opened and closed, Lucky strolled into the office whistling.

"Where the hell have you been?" Joey began. "Frank's been—"

"Worried?" Lucky spied Jackson. "Hey, bro, heard you got your case solved while I was away. Heard you put Williams behind bars, and got an extra bonus for your trouble. Congratulations on the new job. I hear there's going to be a wedding, too."

"I suppose you were as surprised as the rest of us to learn it was Stud Williams?" Jackson asked.

"Not really. Never trust a two-faced cop." Lucky took the chair facing Joey. "Speaking of Williams—" he reached into his pocket and tossed a picture on the shiny desk "—picked something up for you, bro."

For several seconds the room was quiet, then all at once Joey was on his feet. "Where did you get this picture?"

"I took it."

"Where."

"Key West, Florida."

"She's there?"

"That's right."

When Joe released a string of Italian that left a trail of blue smoke, Jackson sauntered to the desk to eye the picture. Holy hell, he thought. Lucky had located Rhea Williams.

"How did you find her?" Joey snapped. "Or did you know where she was all along?"

Lucky got to his feet. "Don't be crazy, Joey. I only learned where she was a few days ago. I had a hunch and I played it. It took me a few more days to put all the facts together for you, but in the end, you got your answer to that nagging question you've been living with for three years."

Suddenly the fight went out of Joe. "I need a drink."

"I'll pour," Jackson offered.

As Lucky and Joe straddled bar stools, Jackson poured Macallan Scotch for all three of them from behind the bar. Lucky said, "Rhea's been living there since she left Chicago. She lives on a private estate."

"How did you find her?" Jackson asked.

"I'll get into that later. The important thing is I found her and..."

"And?" Joe had already downed his glass of Scotch. He motioned to Jackson to pour him another.

Lucky slid his hand into his leather jacket pocket and pulled out another picture and laid it on the bar. The picture was of Rhea walking along a sandy beach holding onto the hand of a little dark-haired boy no older that three.

The minute Joe's eyes fastened on the picture, he said, "Whose kid, Lucky?"

The question hung in the silence for a full minute. Then finally, Lucky said, "Who does he look like, bro?"

Jackson angled his head to look at the kid and nearly choked on his Scotch. The boy looked like he could be Joe's twin.

"Are you saying he's mine? That she was pregnant when she left town? That I have a son I didn't know about?"

His gaze dropped to the picture and he examined it more closely. Jackson watched as Joey's fingers brushed over the little boy's face several times. "How could she do that?" he whispered. "How could she keep him from me?"

His voice was low, laced with a dangerous quality that hinted of the fury raging inside him.

"Take it easy, Joe," Jackson said. "First you have to make sure he's yours before you get—"

"He is," Lucky confirmed. "That's why I was gone a few extra days. I wanted to make sure I didn't come back bearing false gifts."

Jackson poured Joey another Scotch. "Here, bro. Down another one of these. I'll keep 'em coming." He glanced at Lucky. "You want another one?"

"No. I figure I'll be flying a plane out of here before morning, headed for the Atlantic. At least one of us ought to have a clear head."

An hour later Jackson stepped off the elevator. Joe was working toward a serious drunk, one Jackson couldn't blame him for. But he wasn't worried. It was time Joe faced the past. And Lucky had promised to be his brother's shadow for the next couple of days while Joe pulled it together. And he would pull it together—Joe was the logical one. He never did anything without thinking it through.

As he headed across the bridge to Silks, he noticed a crowd had gathered in front of the display window. Suddenly a little nervous, he shouldered his way through the crowd, then jerked to a stop as his eyes locked on Mac. Standing inside the window he'd placed himself between the beautiful mannequin and Sunni's lion. His hackles were raised an inch off his back, and his canines were gleaming in the spotlight.

"Oh, hell," Jackson muttered. He'd told Sunni just last night that Mac hadn't chewed up or broken anything in more than a week. Before he could get through the crowd, Mac sprang and fur went flying. He reached the door seconds later intending to rescue the lion, but when Sunni spied him and started to come toward him, he quickly changed direction. Hooking onto her arm, he pulled her close and stole a kiss.

Seconds later, she glanced at the crowd that had collected outside the door. "What's going on out there?"

"Let's go in your office, honey."

As he tugged her along, she glanced over her shoulder. "Have you seen Mac? He was here just a minute ago."

"He's entertaining a few people out in the lobby." Jackson waved to Mary as he opened the office door and ushered Sunni inside. "About that lion in the display window. Ever thought about changing the theme?"

"Of course not, silly. I shelled out five thousand big ones for him. Leo is Silks' mascot."

Jackson winced. He should have known the lion was the real deal. Sunni wouldn't wanted a fake-fur mascot.

"Jack...you look a little pale."

"Come here and kiss me, Sis." He drew her against him and nuzzled her lips. Fingering the buttons on her melon-colored silk suit jacket, he whispered, "The twins want to come out and say hi. You know we never did get around to making love on your desk." He reached behind his back and locked the door. "How about it? Let's make a memory. One I'll be able to feed off of for the next few days."

She kissed him and arched her breasts into his hands. "A few days? Are you going somewhere, Jack?"

"Not any distance. Have you heard the weather forecast for the next couple of days? Is it suppose to rain all weekend?"

"And possibly snow. But that shouldn't matter. Not unless you're planning on camping outside."

She unbuttoned his shirt and kissed his bare chest with her hot little mouth. When she unzipped his jeans, he squeezed his eyes shut in anticipation, and decided that the last thing he was going to think about at the moment was flying fur or sleeping on the terrace in bad weather. Pneumonia and anteing up five grand for a new mascot was a small price to pay for a touch of heaven. And Sunni's touch was pure heaven.

He really should confess just how much power she had over him. Tell her how much he liked her hands on him, touching and stroking. Massaging and tugging, and...

No, they were past words now. She was out of her skirt and he was definitely out of his jeans—in a matter of speaking.

Deciding to show Sunni instead, Jackson lifted her into his arms and headed for the desk.

* * * * *

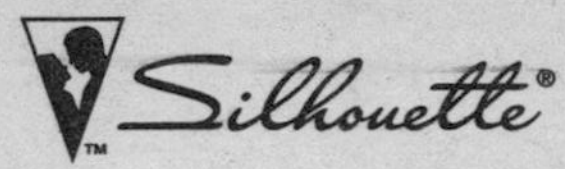

INTIMATE MOMENTS®

COMING NEXT MONTH

#1159 LAWMAN'S REDEMPTION—Marilyn Pappano
Heartbreak Canyon
Canyon County Undersheriff Brady Marshall hadn't planned on fatherhood, but when fourteen-year-old Les came to town claiming to be his daughter, his plans changed. Alone and in danger, Les needed help and—more important—a family. And Brady needed his old flame Hallie Madison to make that happen....

#1160 HER LORD PROTECTOR—Eileen Wilks
Romancing the Crown
Visions of a troubled woman had haunted psychic Rosalinda Giaberti's mind ever since the moment she first saw the prince of Montebello. Rosie wanted to warn him, but there were those who would stop at nothing to keep her from him. It was up to Lord Drew Harrington to protect Rosie, but could he do that without risking his own heart?

#1161 THE BLACK SHEEP'S BABY—Kathleen Creighton
Into the Heartland
When Eric Lanagan came home for Christmas with an infant daughter, his family was shocked! They didn't know about the baby's true parents or her tragic past—a past shared by her aunt, Devon O'Rourke. Eric was falling in love with Devon, and he knew that the only way to keep his daughter was to make Devon remember the childhood she'd worked so hard to forget....

#1162 COWBOY UNDER COVER—Marilyn Tracy
Who was terrorizing the New Mexico ranch that city slicker Jeannie Wasserman had bought as a home for orphans? Undercover federal marshal Chance Salazar was sure it was the elusive *El Patrón*. Determined to catch his criminal, Chance got hired on as a cowboy and was prepared for anything—except his growing desire for Jeannie.

#1163 SWEET REVENGE—Nina Bruhns
Muse Summerfield was the hottest thing in New Orleans—until she disappeared. That was when her twin sister, Grace, and police detective Auri "Creole" Levalois began burning up Bourbon Street in an effort to find her. Creole believed that Muse held the key to his foster brother's murder, but would he and Grace survive their search?

#1164 BACHELOR IN BLUE JEANS—Lauren Nichols
High school sweethearts Kristin Chase and Zach Davis once had big dreams for their future, dreams that never came to pass. Years later, a suspicious death in their hometown brought Zach and Kristin back together. Surrounded by mystery and danger, they realized that they needed each other now more than ever.

SIMCNM0602